Dua Before Studying!

للَّهُمَّ انْفَعْنِي بِمَا عَلَّمْتَنِي وَ عَلِّمْنِي مَا يَنْفَعُنِي

.اللَّهُمَّ إِنِّي أَسْأَلُكَ فَهمَ النَّبِيِّينَ وَ حِفْظَ الْمُرْسَلِينَ الْمُقَرَّبِينَ

اللَّهُمَّ اجْعَلْ لِسَانِي عَامِرًا بِذِكْرِكَ وَ قَلْبِي بِخَشْيَتِكَ .

.إِنَّكَ عَلَى مَا تَشَاءُ قَدِيرٌ وَ أَنْتَ حَسْبُنَا اللهُ وَ نِعْمَ الْوَكِيلُ

"ALLAHUMMA INFA'NII BIMAA 'ALLAMTANII WA'ALLIMNII MAA YANFA'UUNII.

ALLAHUMMA INII AS'ALUKA FAHMAL-NABIYYEN WA HIFZAL MURSALEEN AL-MUQARRABEEN.

ALLAHUMMA IJAL LEESANEE 'AIMAN BI DHIKRIKA WA QALBI BI KHASHYATIKA.

INNAKA 'ALA MA-TASHA'U QADEER WA ANTA HASBUN-ALLAHU WA NA'MAL WAKEEL."

OH ALLAH!

MAKE USEFUL FOR ME THAT WHAT YOU HAVE TAUGHT ME AND TEACH ME KNOWLEDGE THAT WILL BE USEFUL TO ME.

OH ALLAH!

I ASK YOU FOR THE UNDERSTANDING OF THE PROPHETS AND THE MEMORY OF THE MESSENGERS, AND THOSE NEAREST TO YOU.

OH ALLAH!

MAKE MY TONGUE FULL OF YOUR REMEMBRANCE AND MY HEART WITH AWE OF YOU.

OH ALLAH!

YOU DO WHATEVER YOU WISH, AND YOU ARE MY AVAILER AND PROTECTOR AND BEST OF AID.

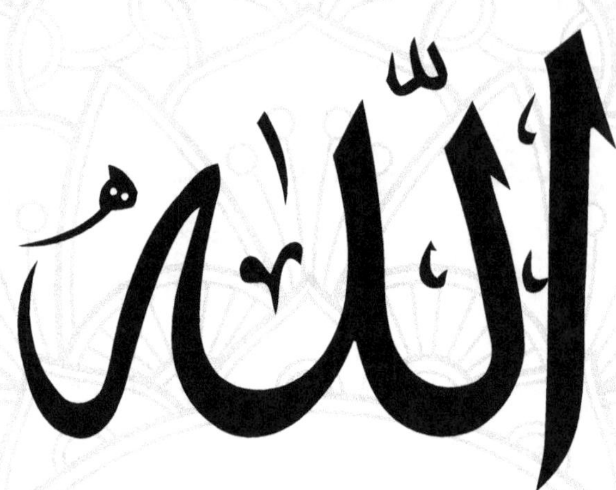

ALLAH

The Only One God

Allah is the Unique Name of God.

The Being Who is perfect in every way, in His knowledge, His power, His wisdom...

He is Allah, other than whom there is no deity, Knower of the unseen and the witnessed. He is the Entirely Merciful, the Especially Merciful.

What Does the Oneness of Allah's Names and Attributes Mean?

Oneness in attributes means that the qualities of the Almighty Allah are His very being and not additional to His being.

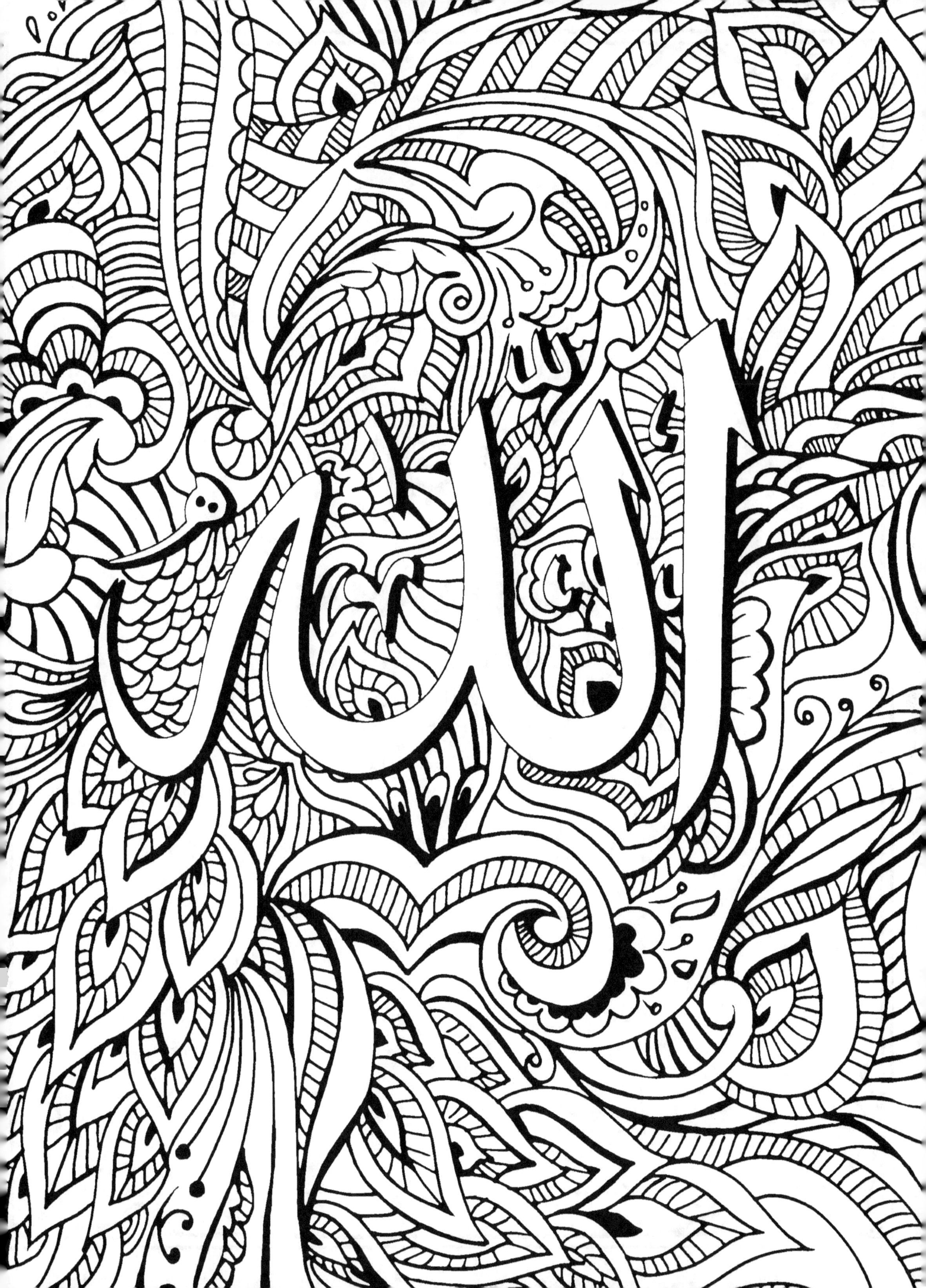

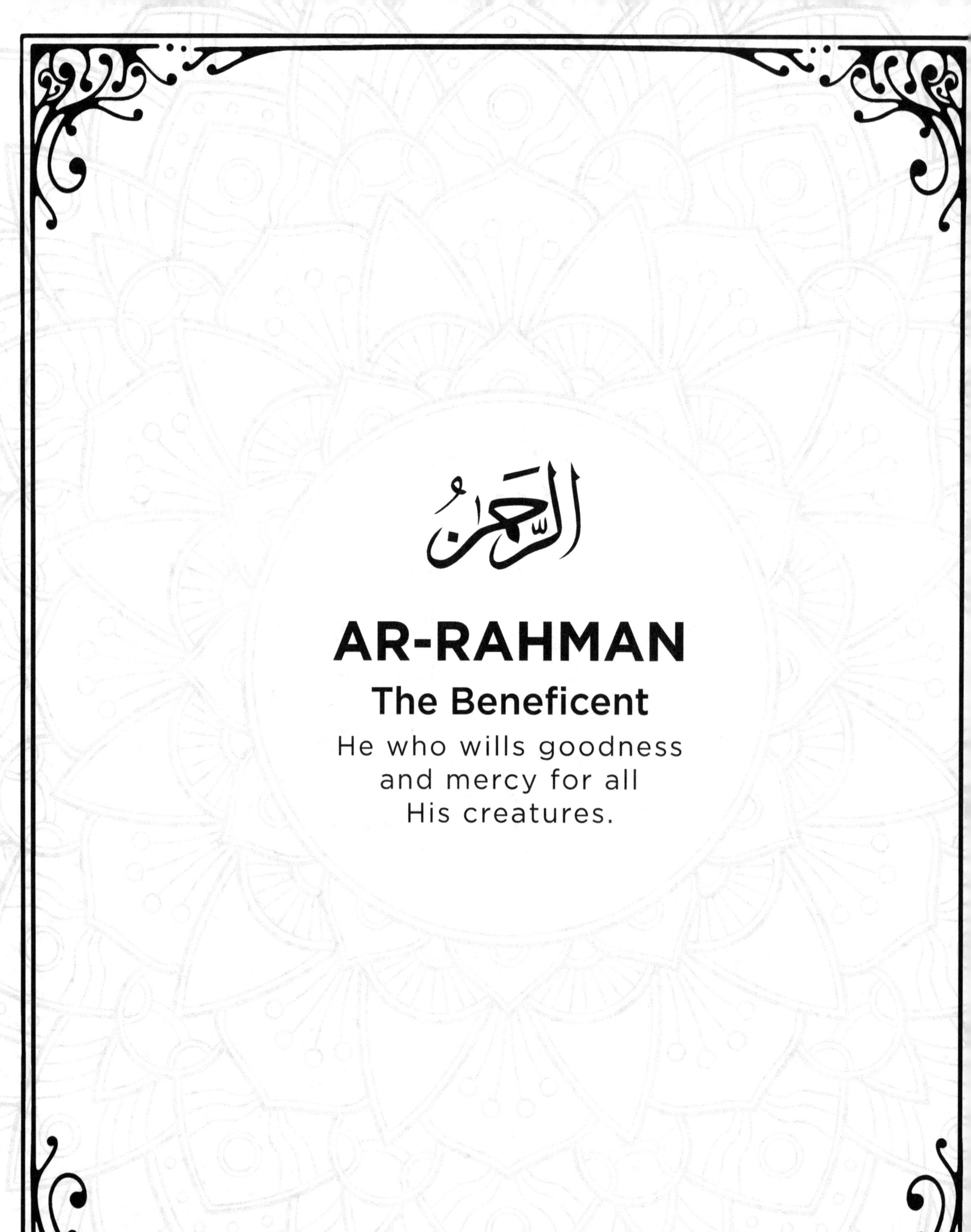

الرَّحْمٰنُ

AR-RAHMAN

The Beneficent

He who wills goodness
and mercy for all
His creatures.

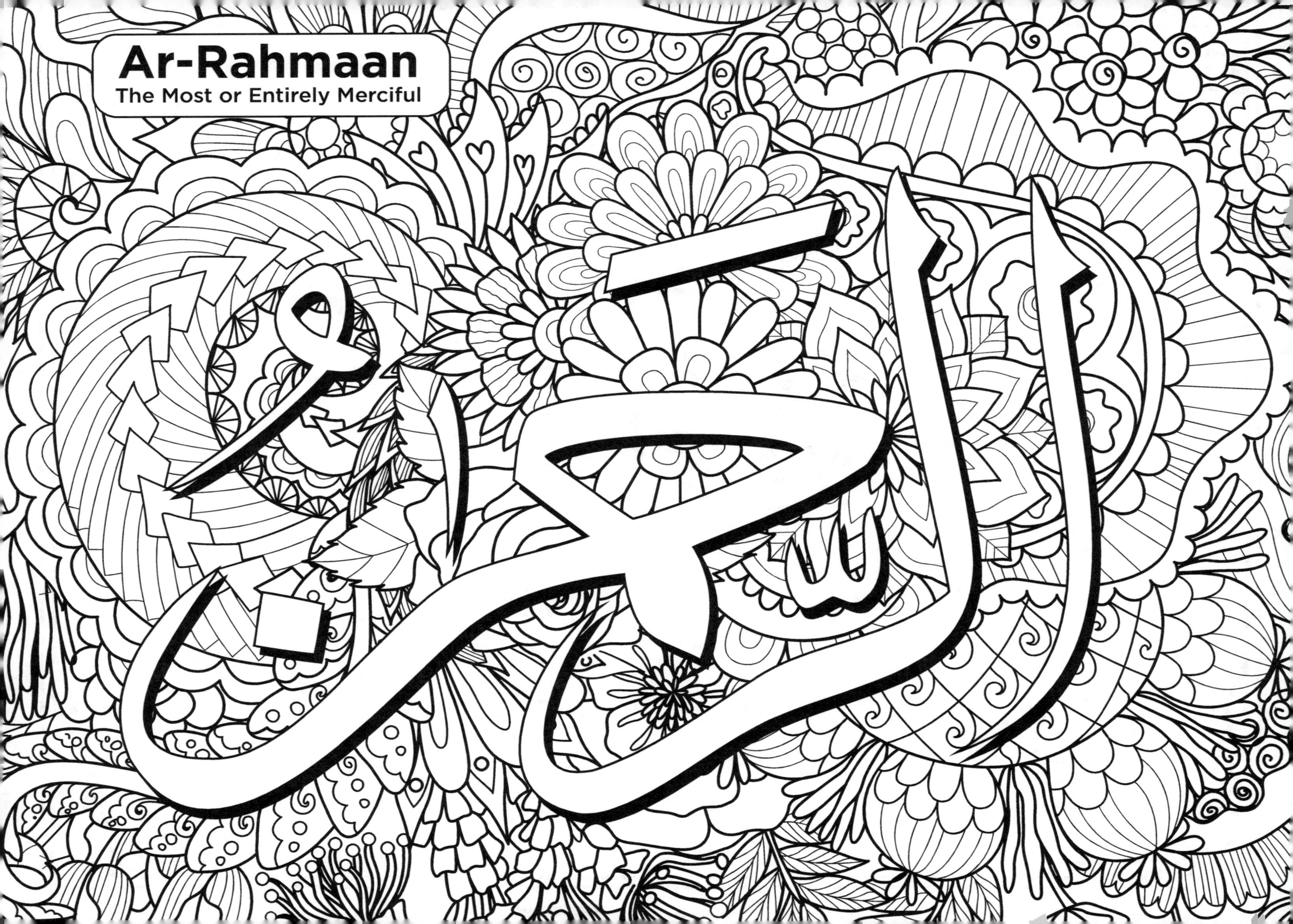
Ar-Rahmaan
The Most or Entirely Merciful

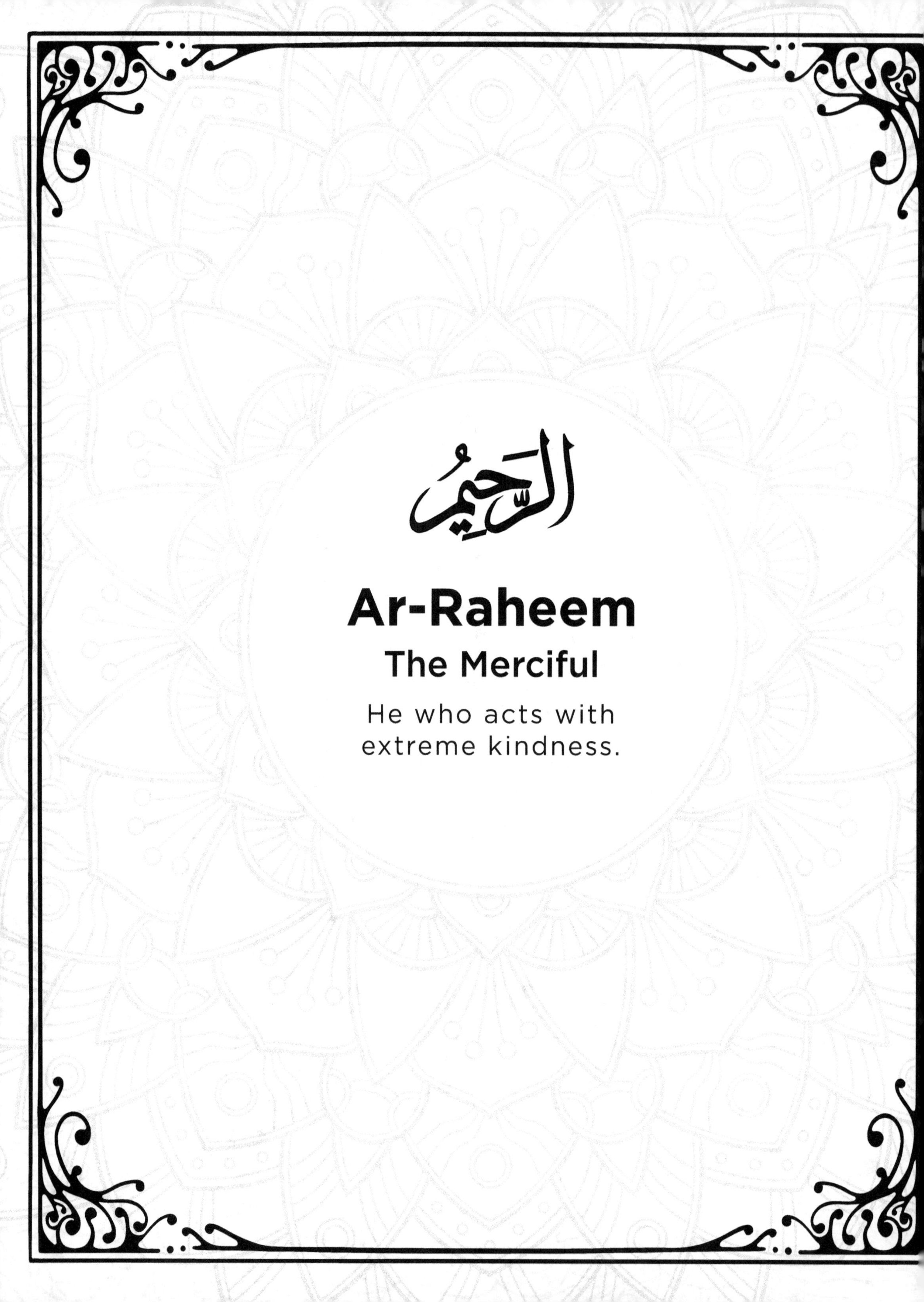

الرَّحِيمُ

Ar-Raheem

The Merciful

He who acts with
extreme kindness.

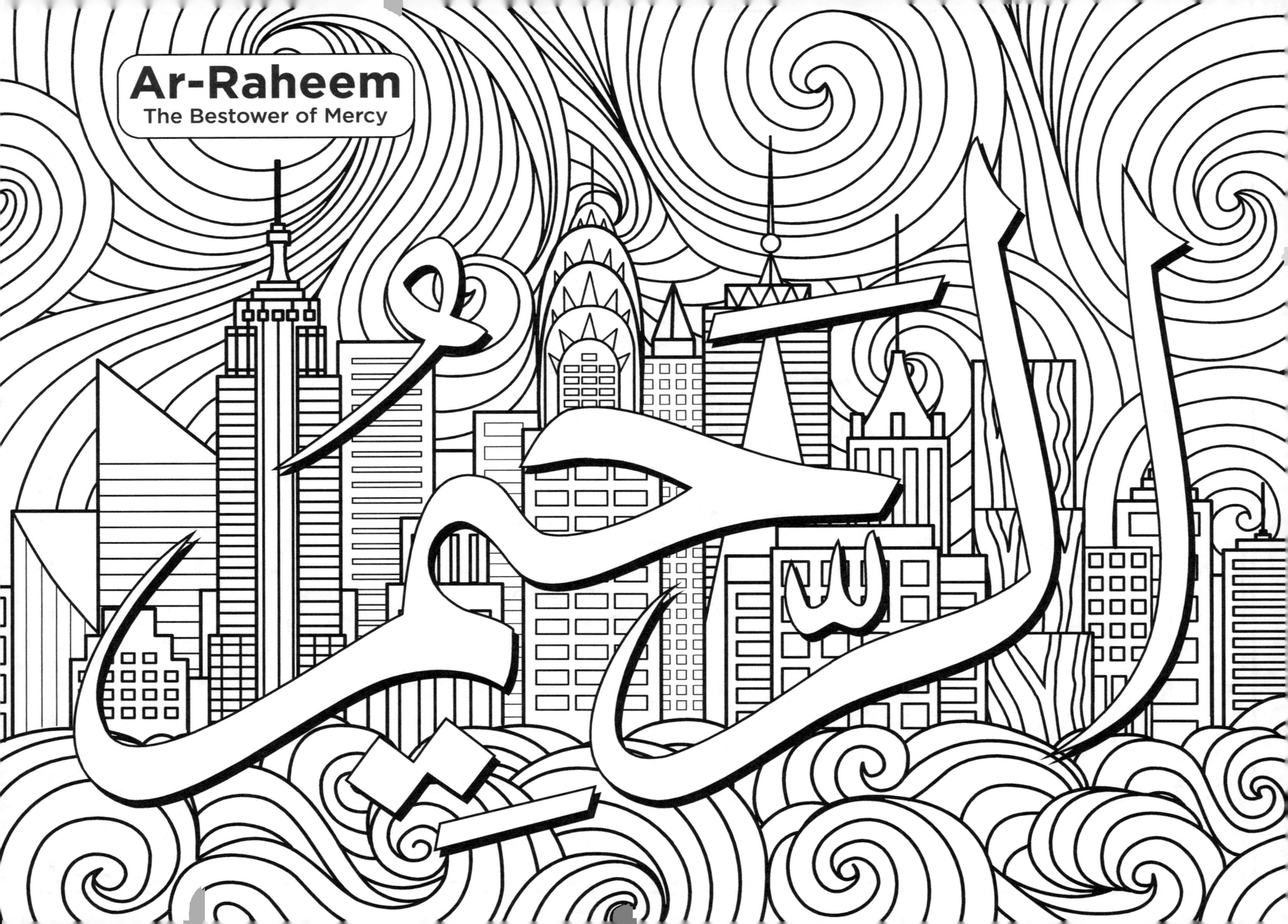
Ar-Raheem
The Bestower of Mercy

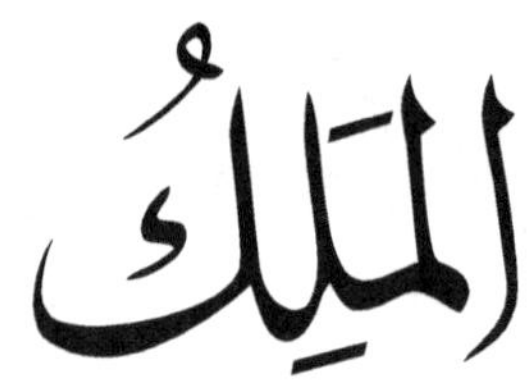

Al-Malik

The Eternal Lord

The Sovereign Lord. The One with the complete Dominion. The One Who's Dominion is clear from imperfection.

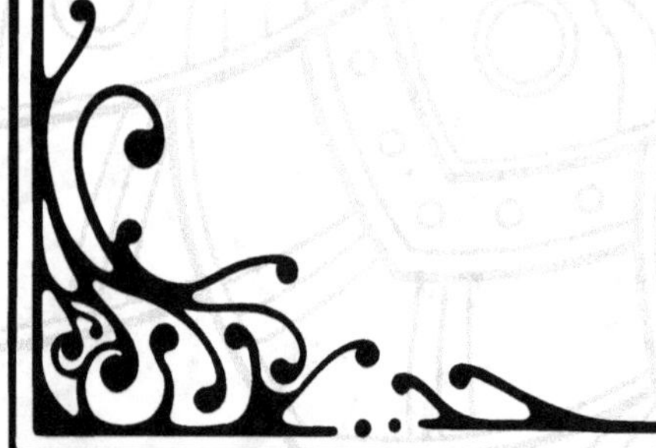

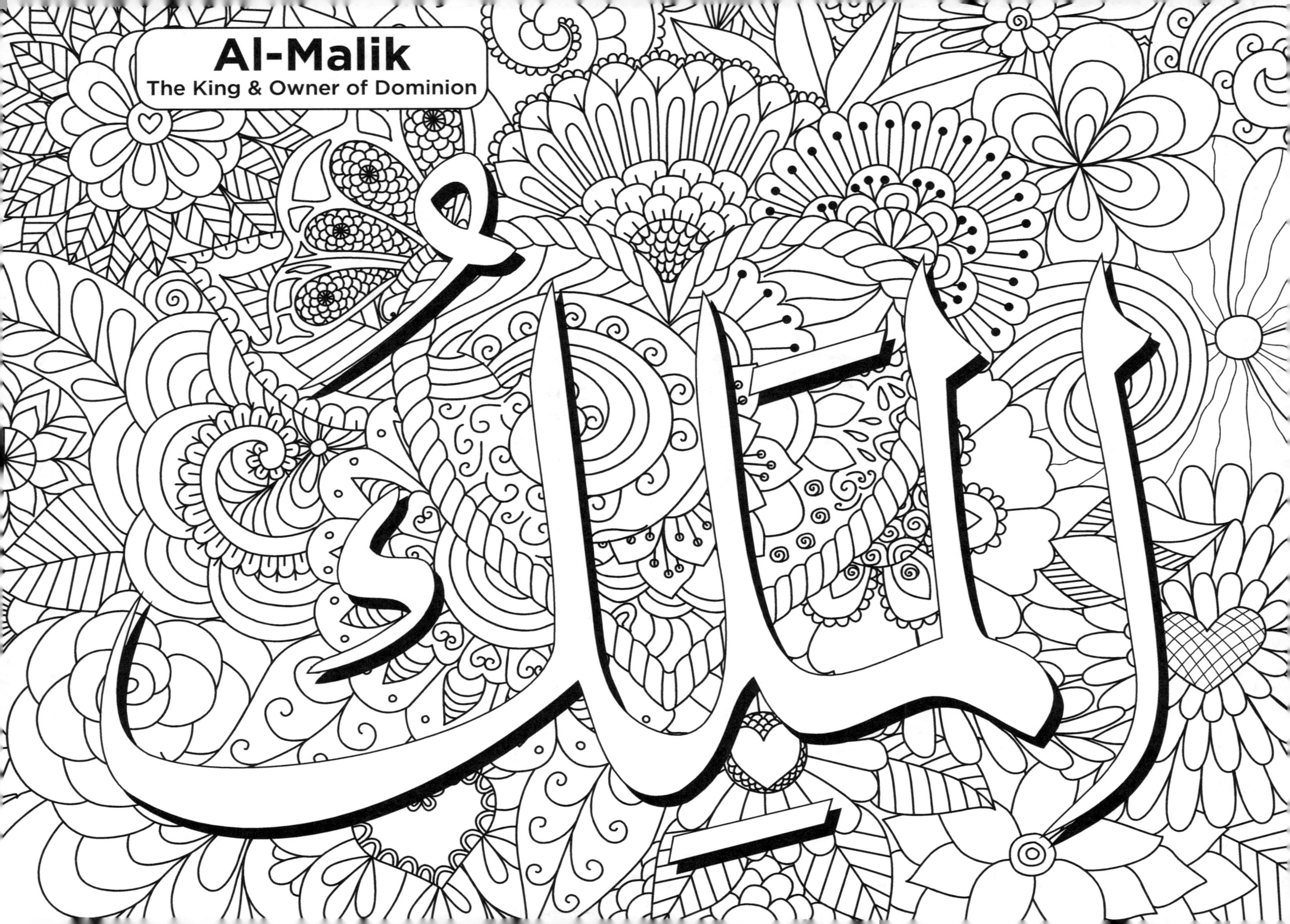
Al-Malik
The King & Owner of Dominion
المَلِكُ

الْقُدُّوسُ

Al-Quddus

The Absolutely Pure

The One who is pure from any imperfection and clear from all assigned partners and adversaries.

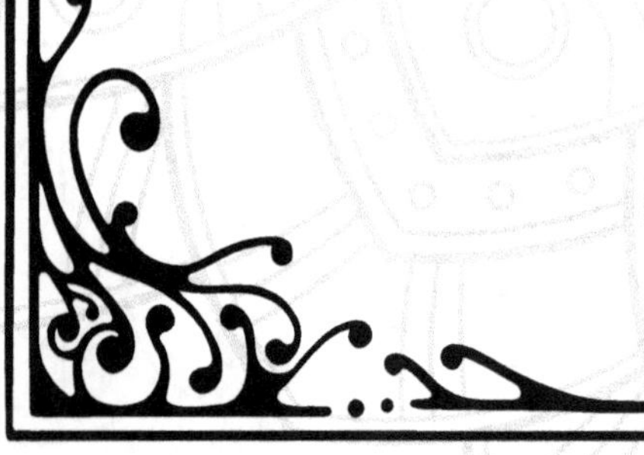

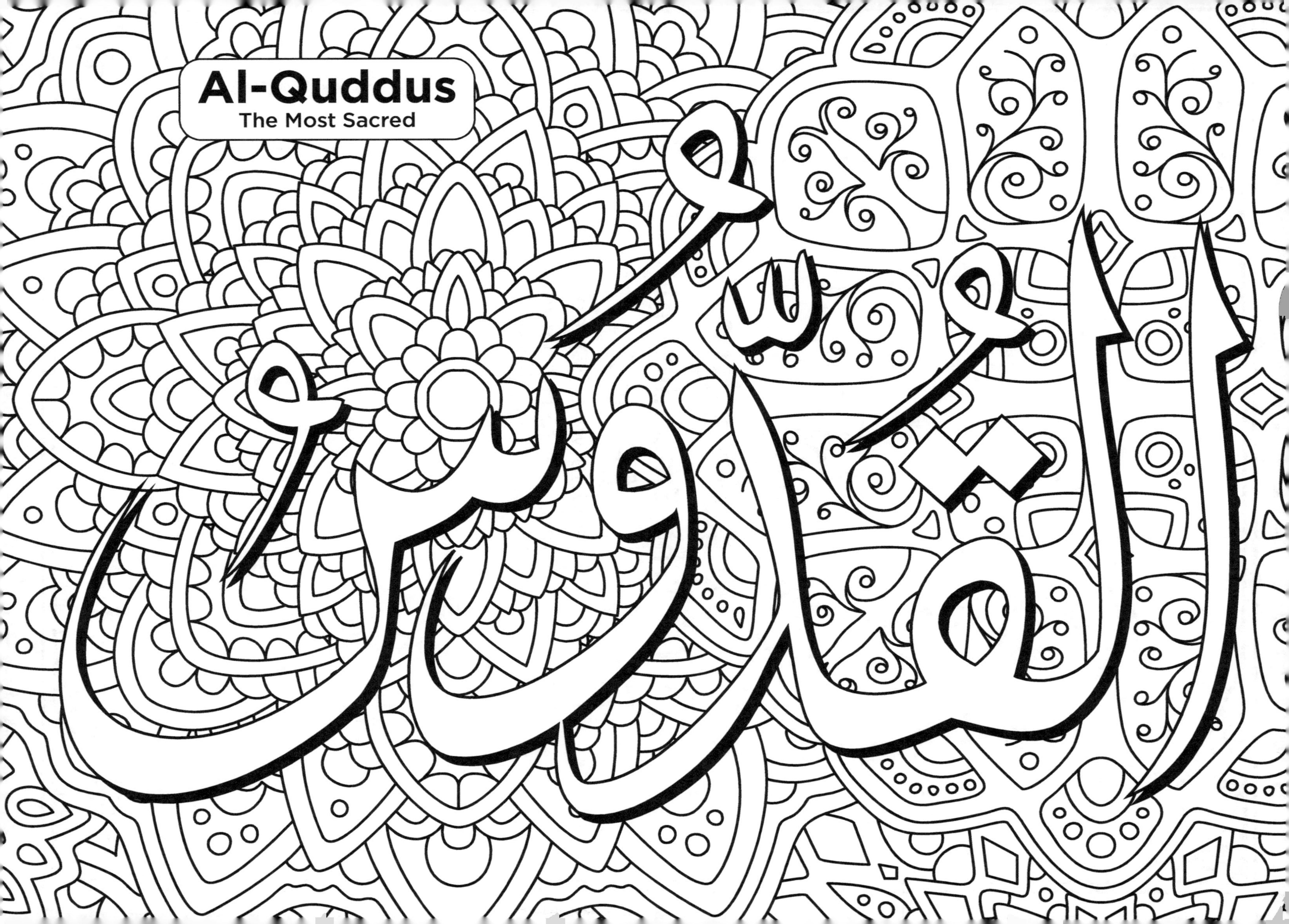
Al-Quddus
The Most Sacred
القدوس

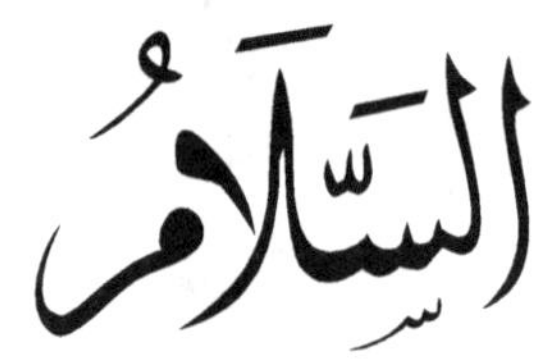

As-Salam

The Embodiment of Peace

The One who is free from defect. The Giver of peace and safety.

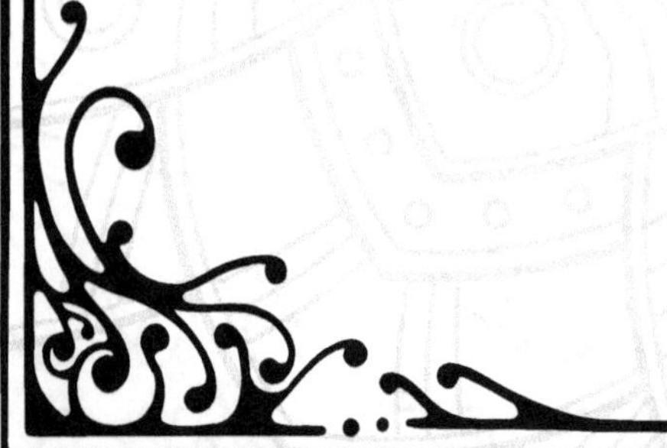

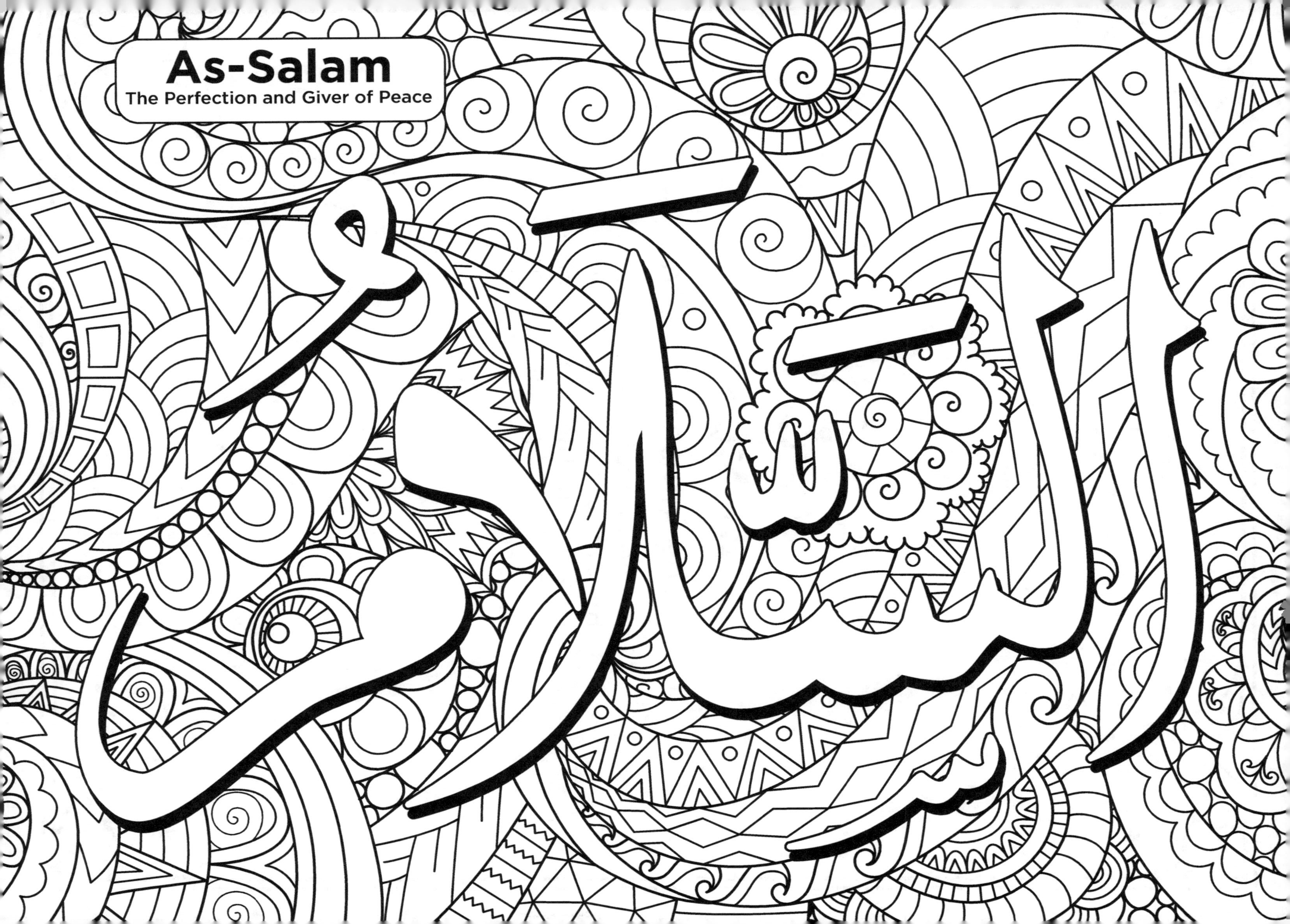
As-Salam
The Perfection and Giver of Peace
ٱلسَّلَامُ

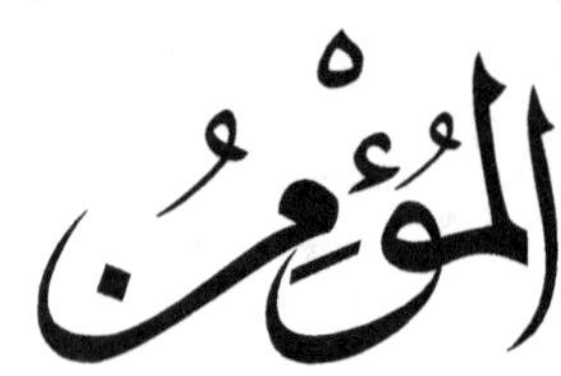

Al-Mu'min

The Infuser of Faith

The One who affirms and believes His Oneness and the One who gives emaan. The One who gives security and peace, and the One who removes fear.

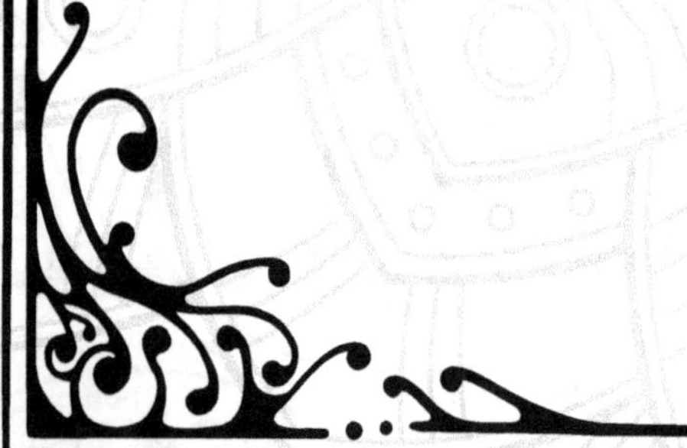

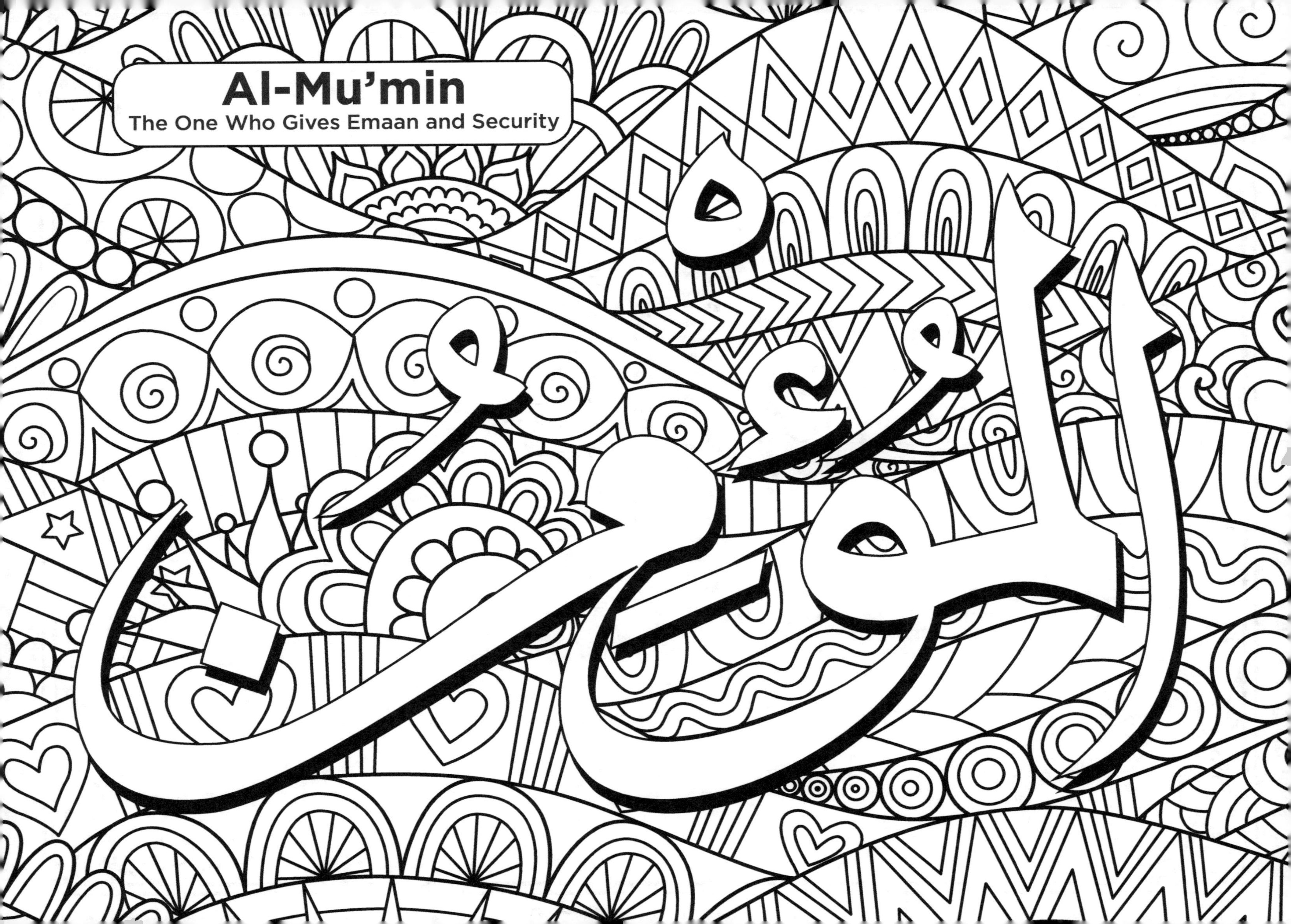
Al-Mu'min
The One Who Gives Emaan and Security
المؤمن

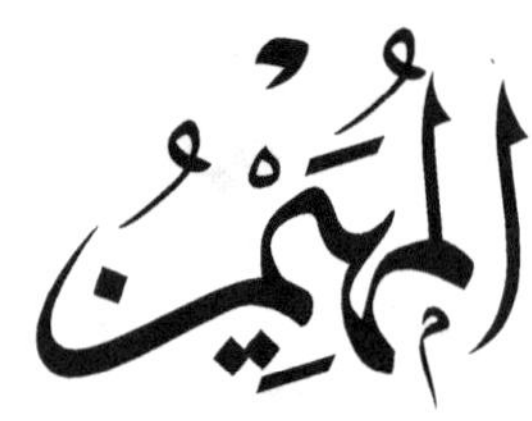

Al-Muhaymin

The Preserver of Safety

The One who witnesses the sayings and deeds of His creatures.

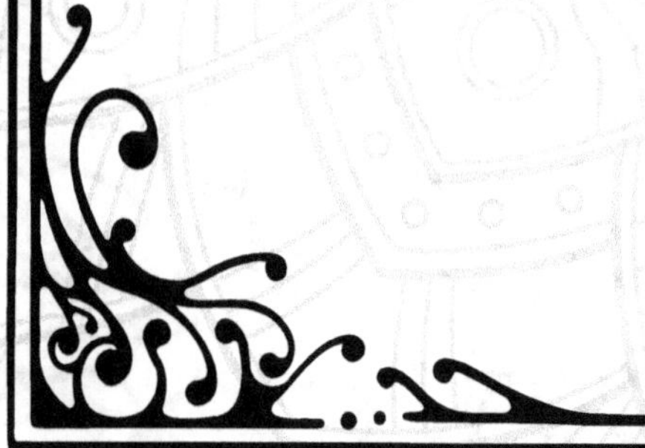

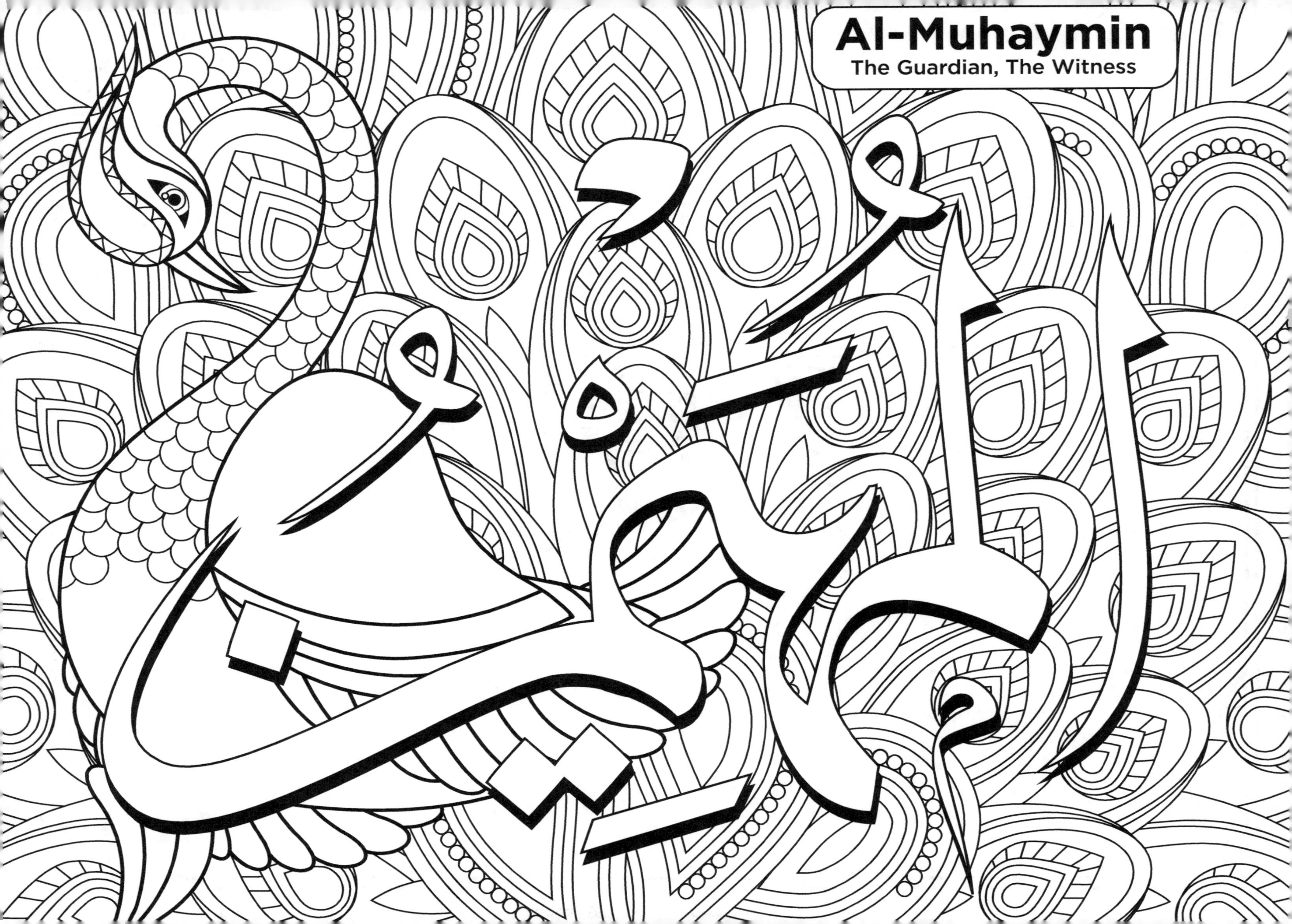
Al-Muhaymin
The Guardian, The Witness

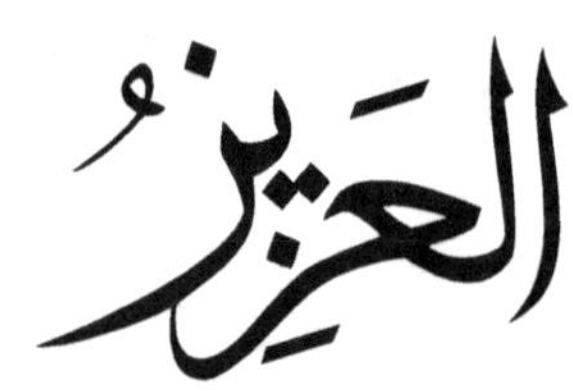

Al-Aziz

The All Mighty

The Strong, The Defeater
who is not defeated.

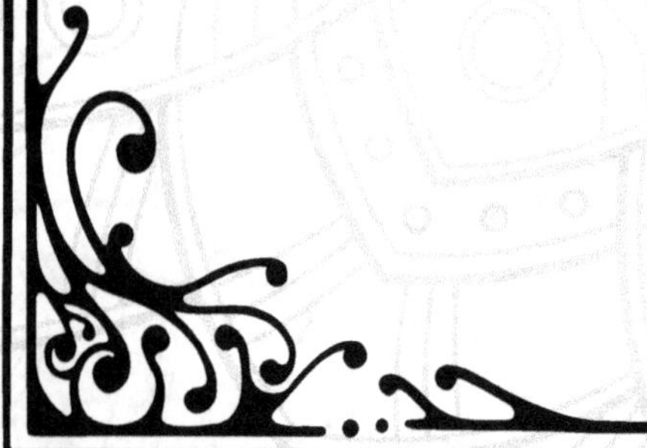

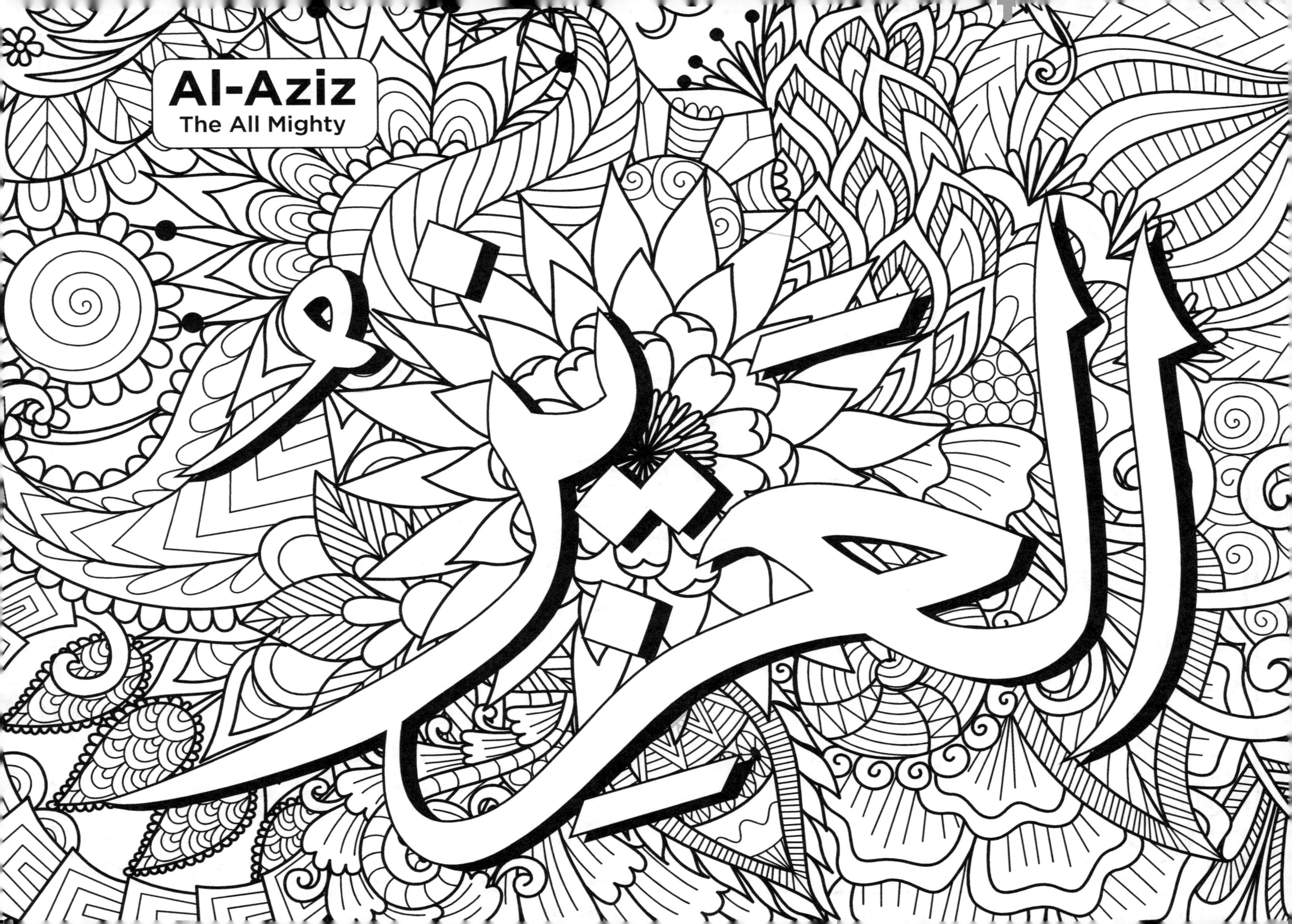
Al-Aziz
The All Mighty
العزيز

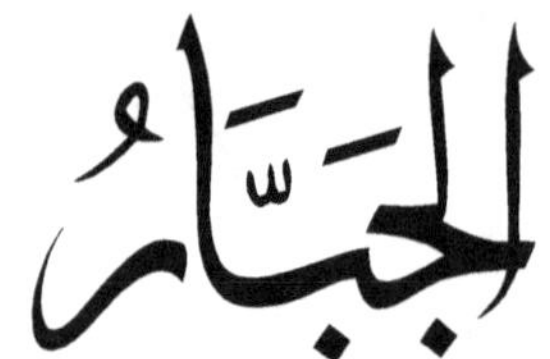

Al-Jabbar

The Compeller

The One who reforms what is broken. Resolver of the affairs of all creatures. Caterer to the needs of all.

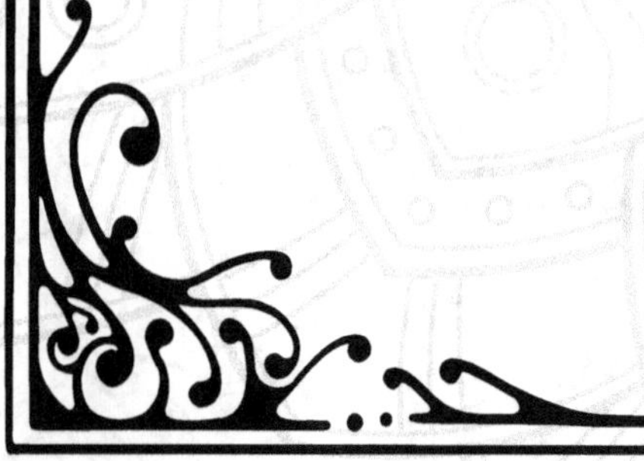

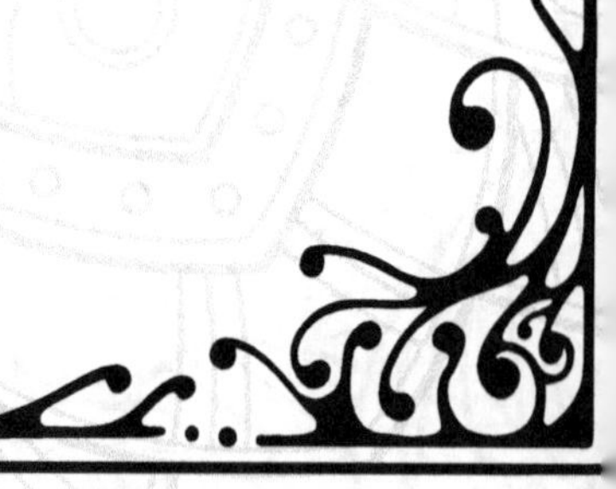

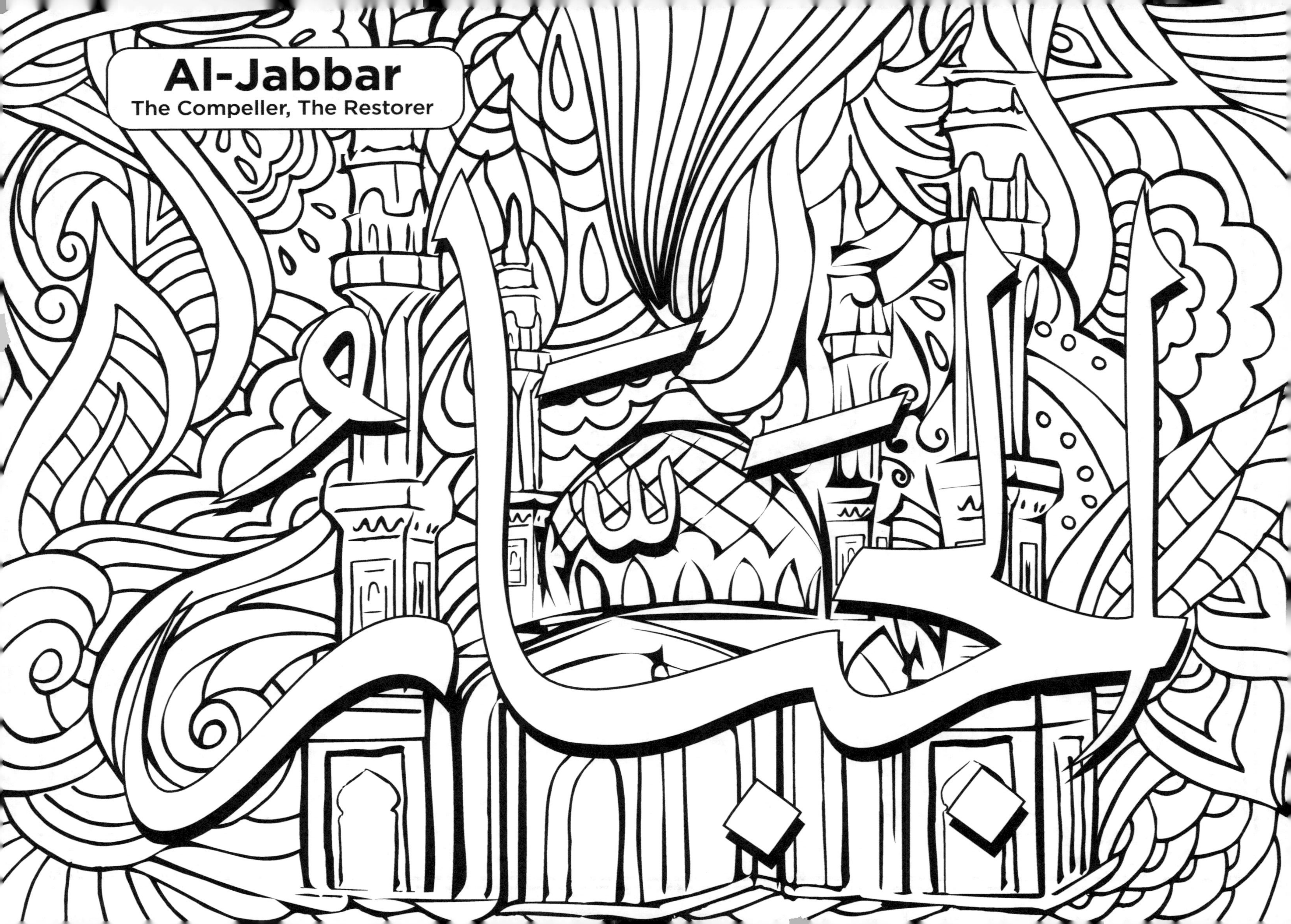
Al-Jabbar
The Compeller, The Restorer

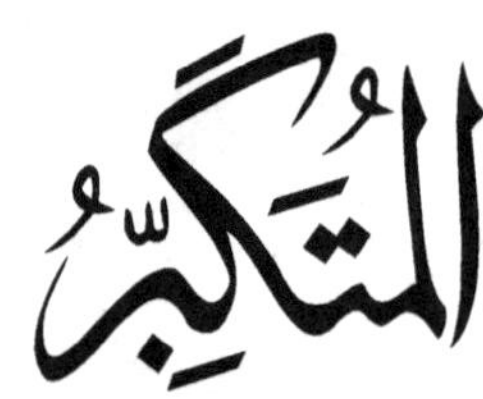

Al-Mutakabbir

The Dominant One

The One who is clear from the attributes of the creatures and from resembling them.

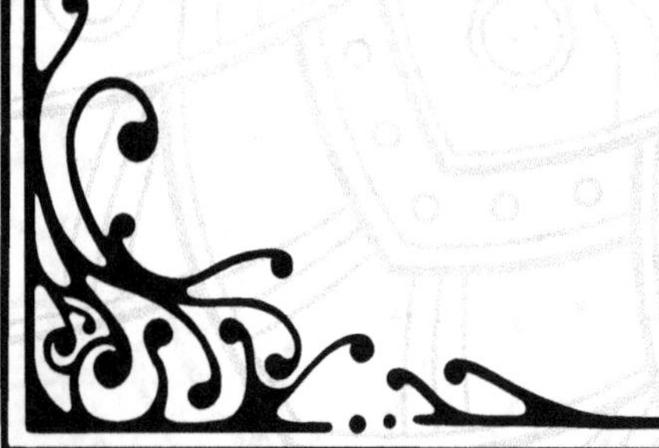

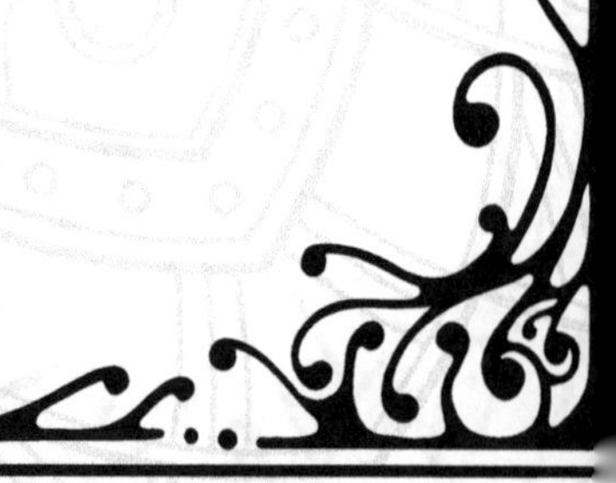

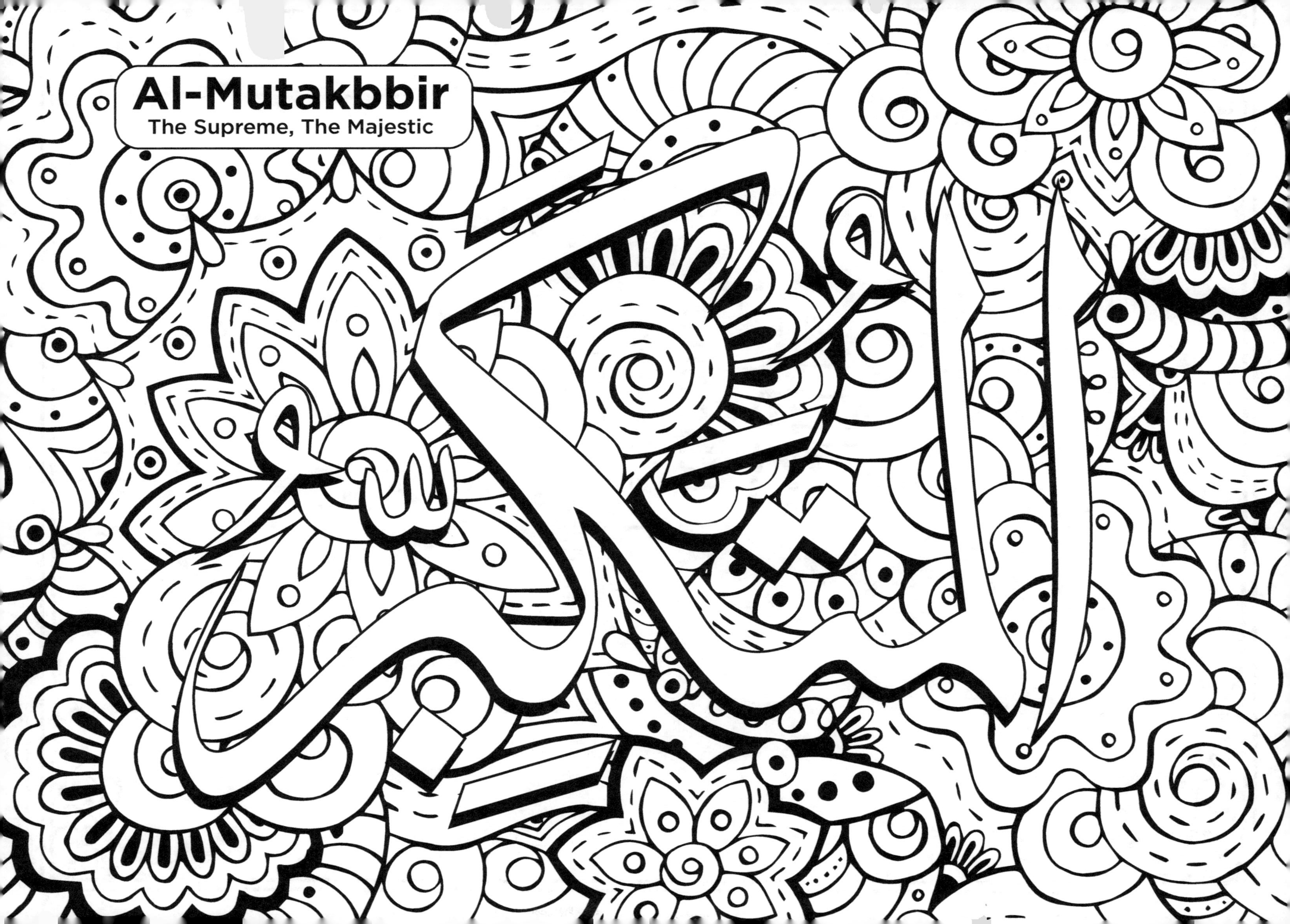
Al-Mutakbbir
The Supreme, The Majestic

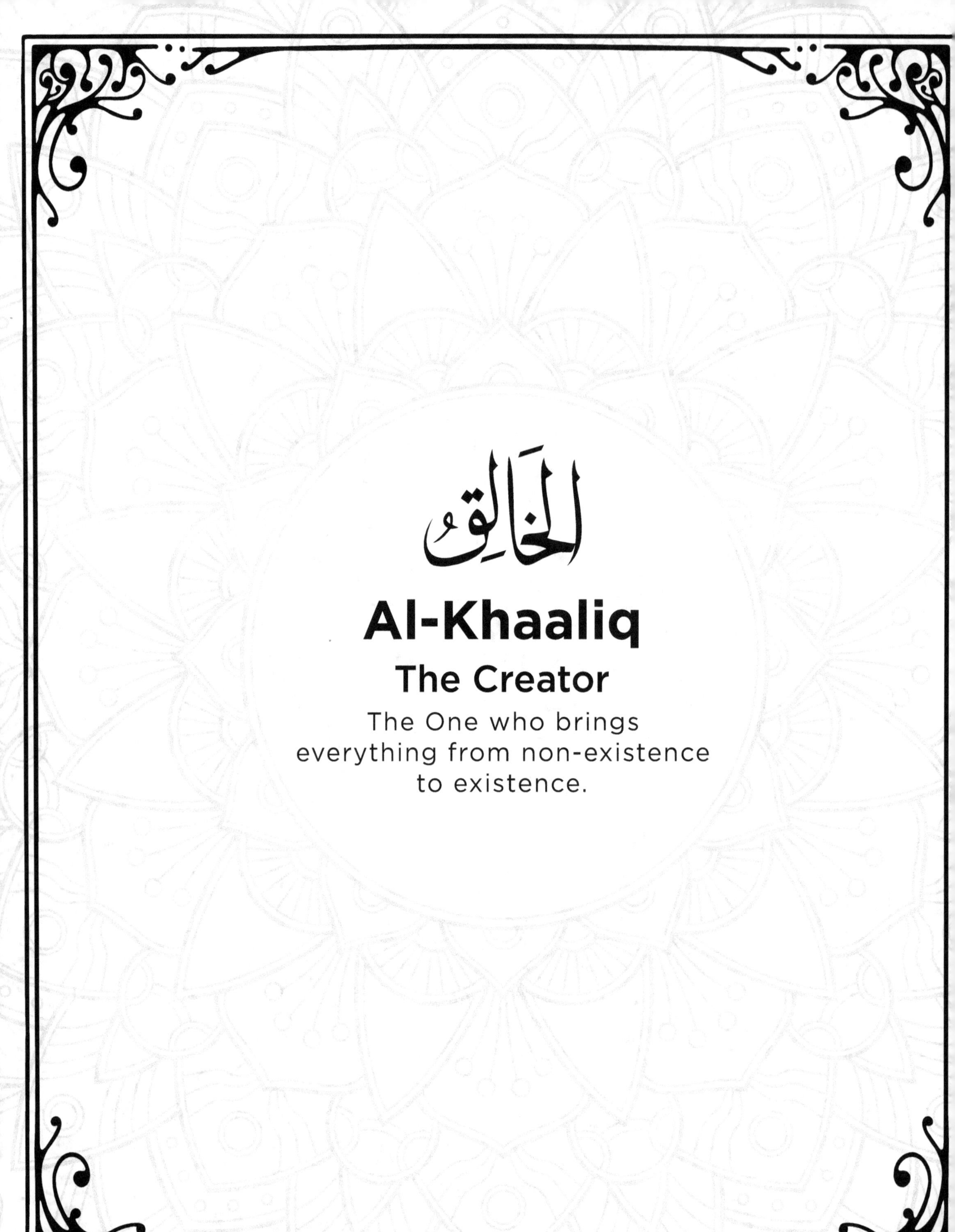

الخَالِق

Al-Khaaliq

The Creator

The One who brings everything from non-existence to existence.

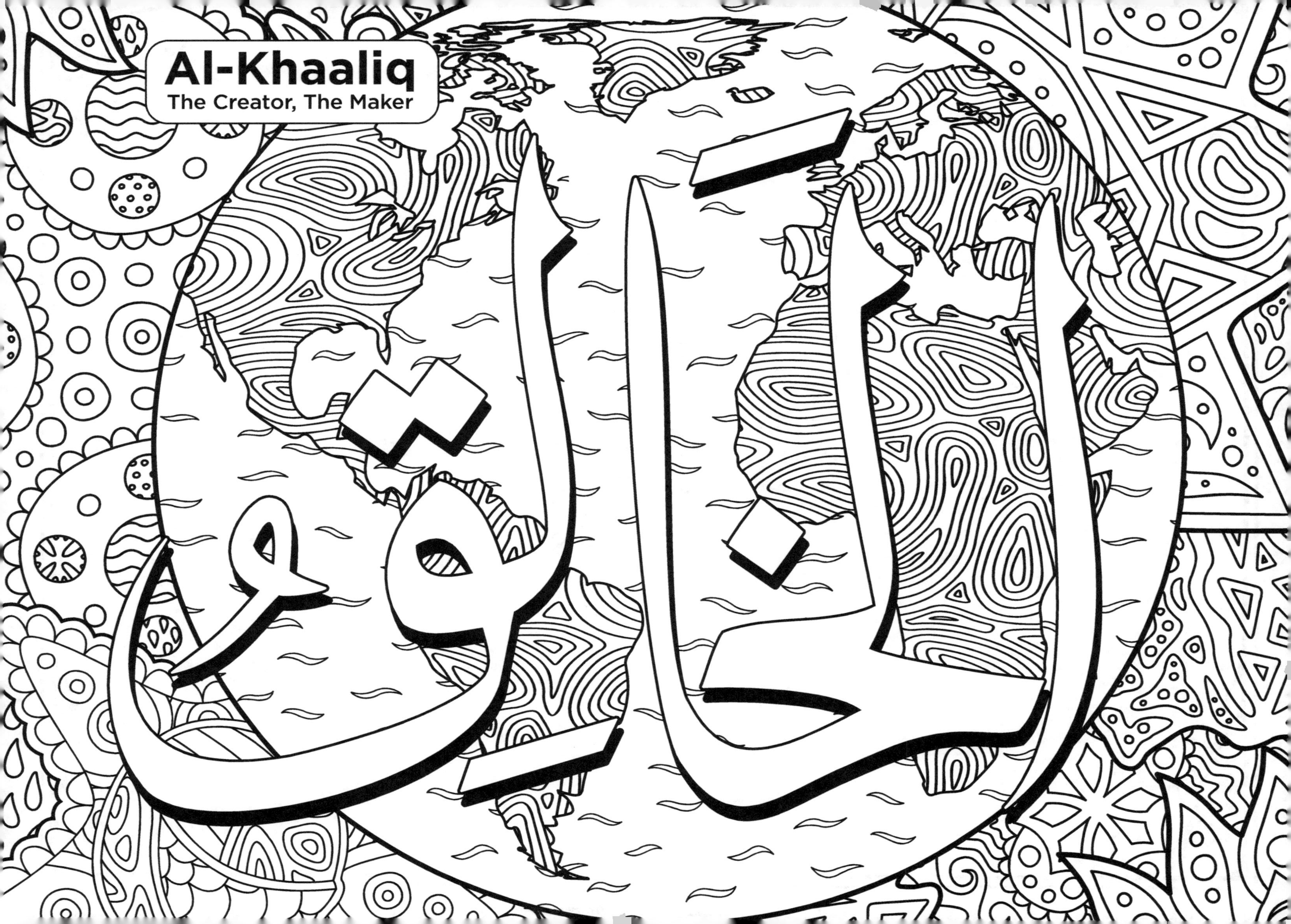
Al-Khaaliq
The Creator, The Maker
الخَالِق

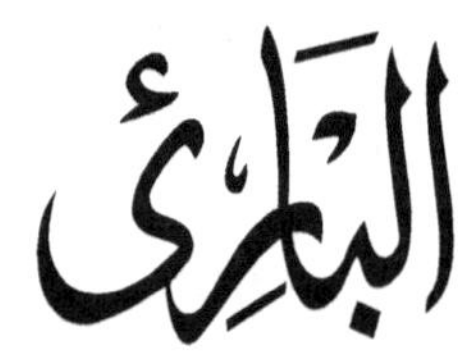

Al-Barri’

The Originator

The Creator who has the power
to turn the entities.

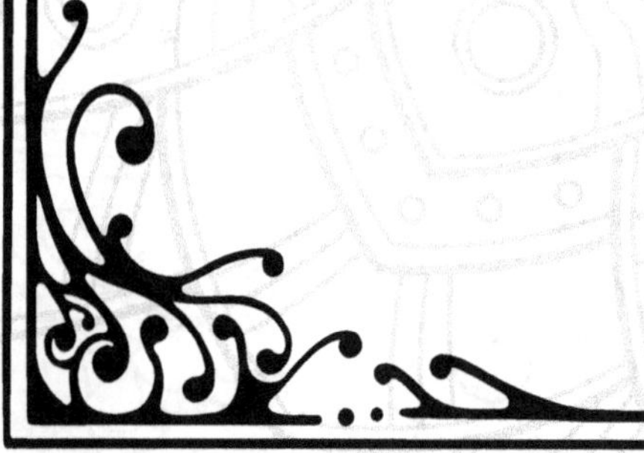

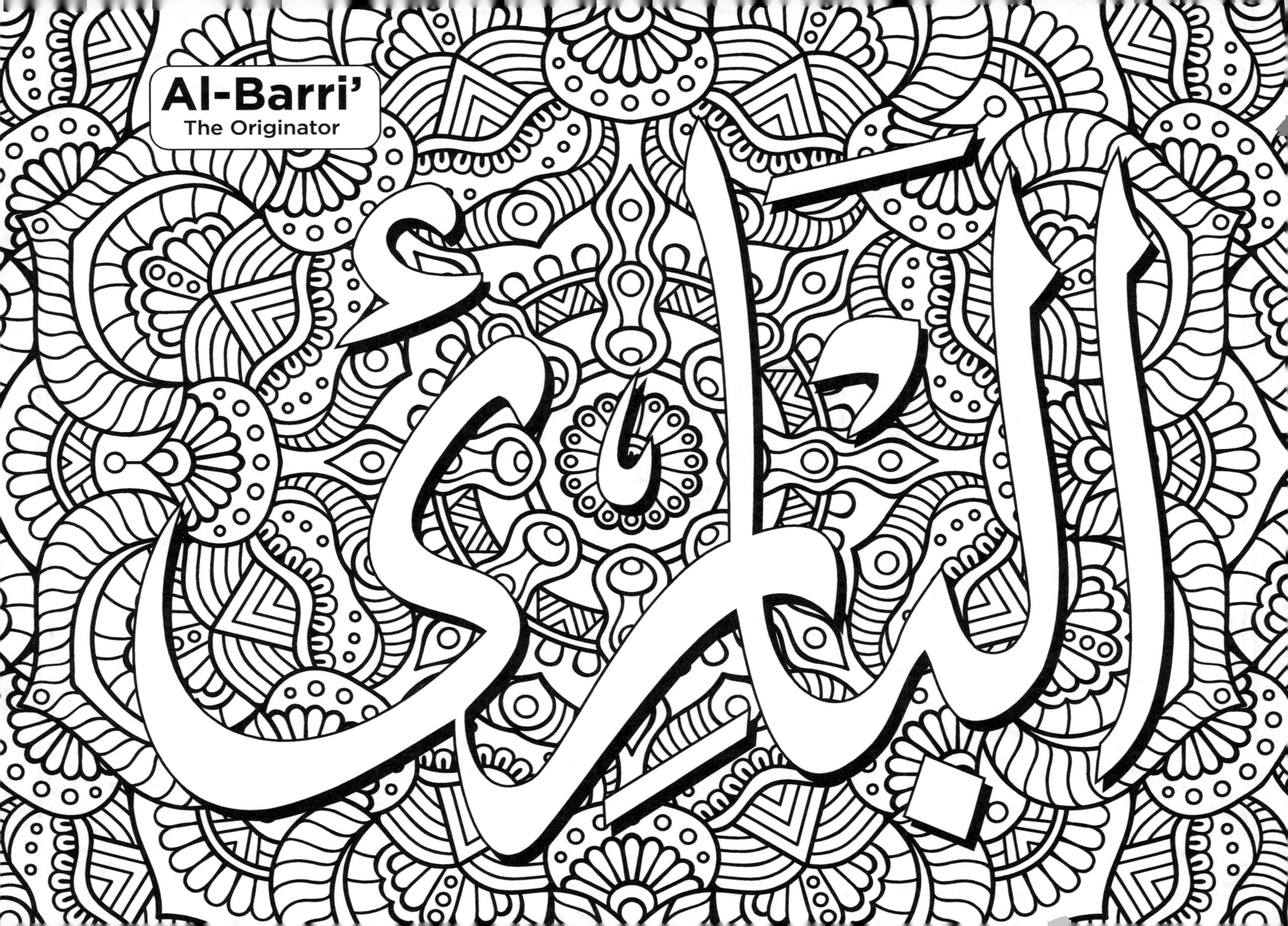
Al-Barri'
The Originator

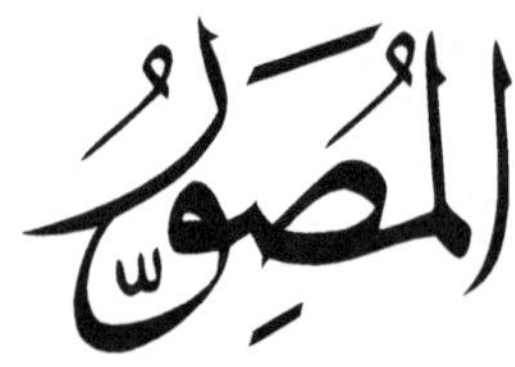

Al-Musawwir

The Fashioner

The One who forms
His creatures in different
shapes and forms.

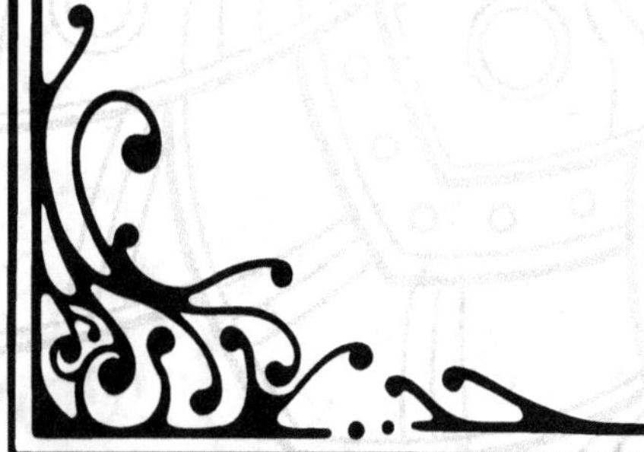

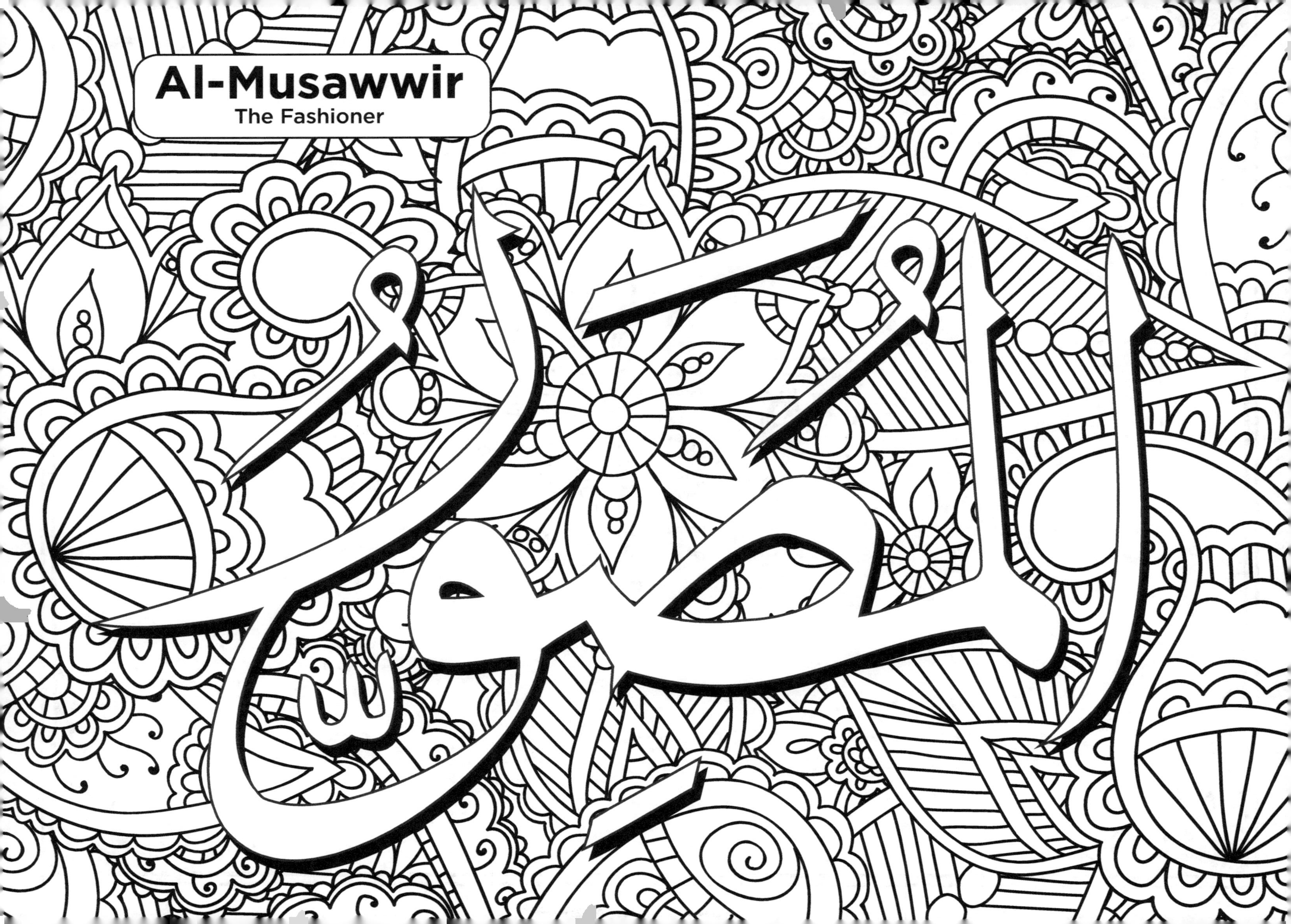
Al-Musawwir
The Fashioner
المصور

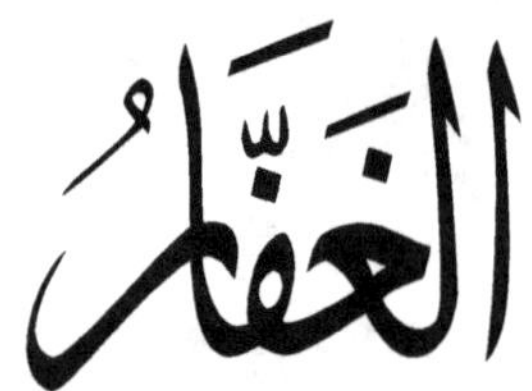

Al-Ghaffaar

The Great Forgiver

The Forgiver, The One who forgives the sins of His slaves time and time again.

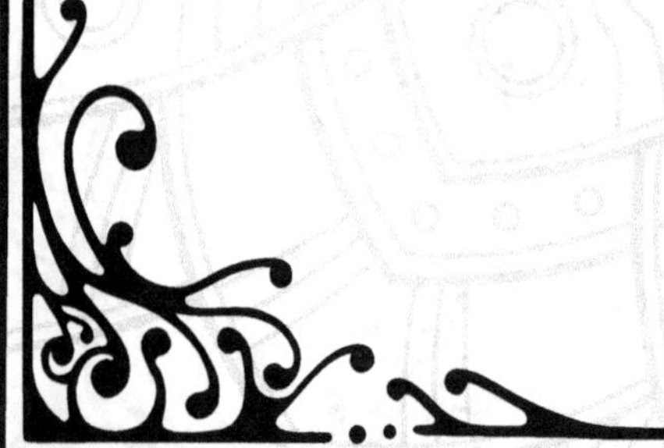

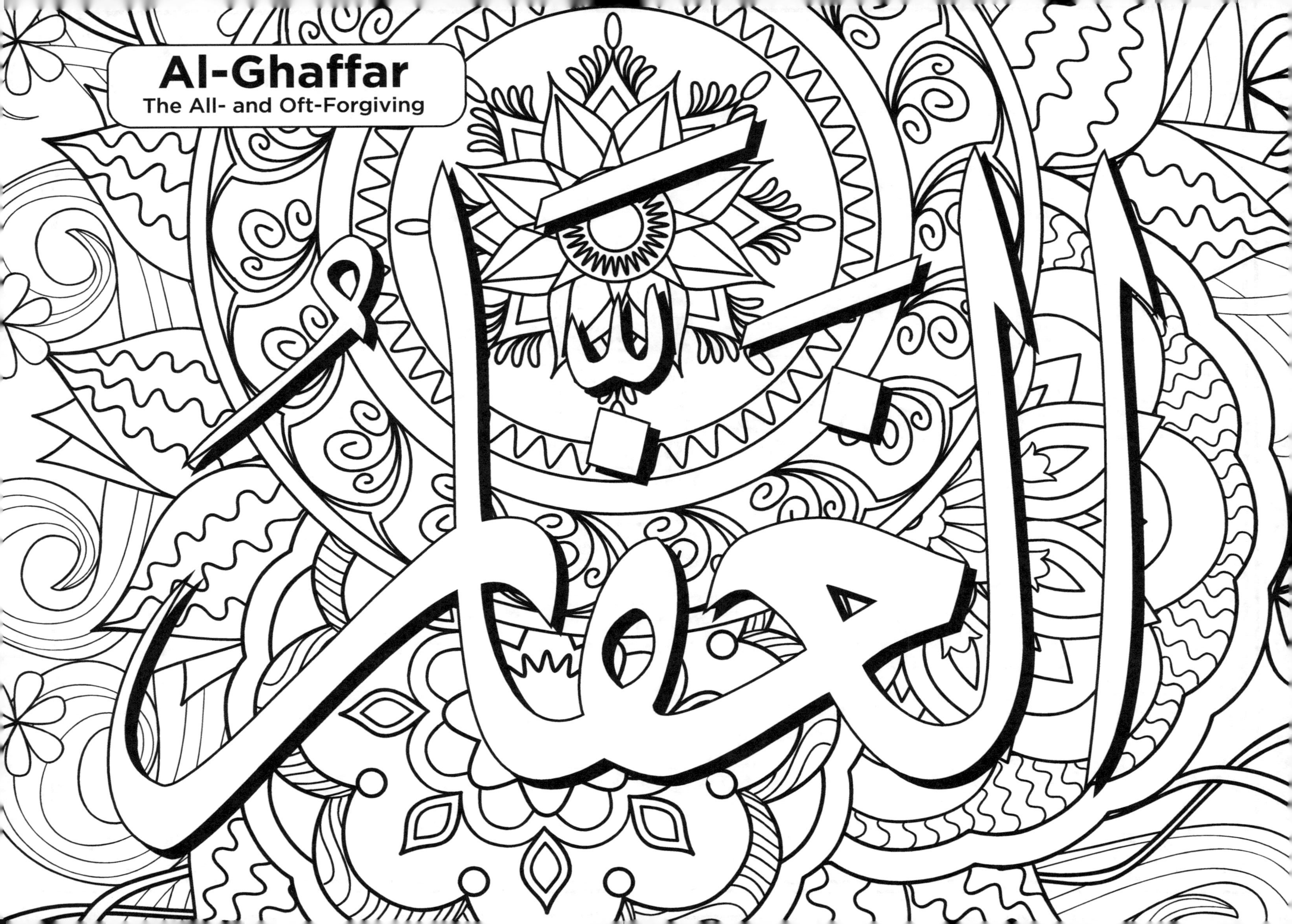

Al-Ghaffar
The All- and Oft-Forgiving
الغفار

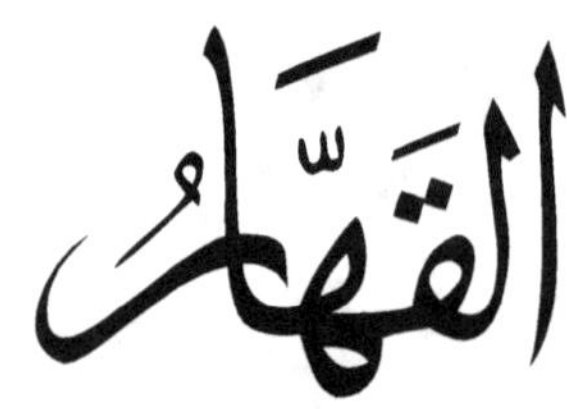

Al-Qahhaar

The All-Prevailing One

The Dominant, The One
who has perfect power.

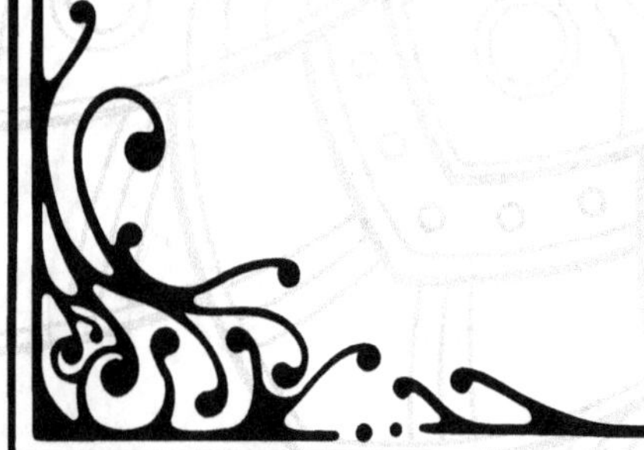

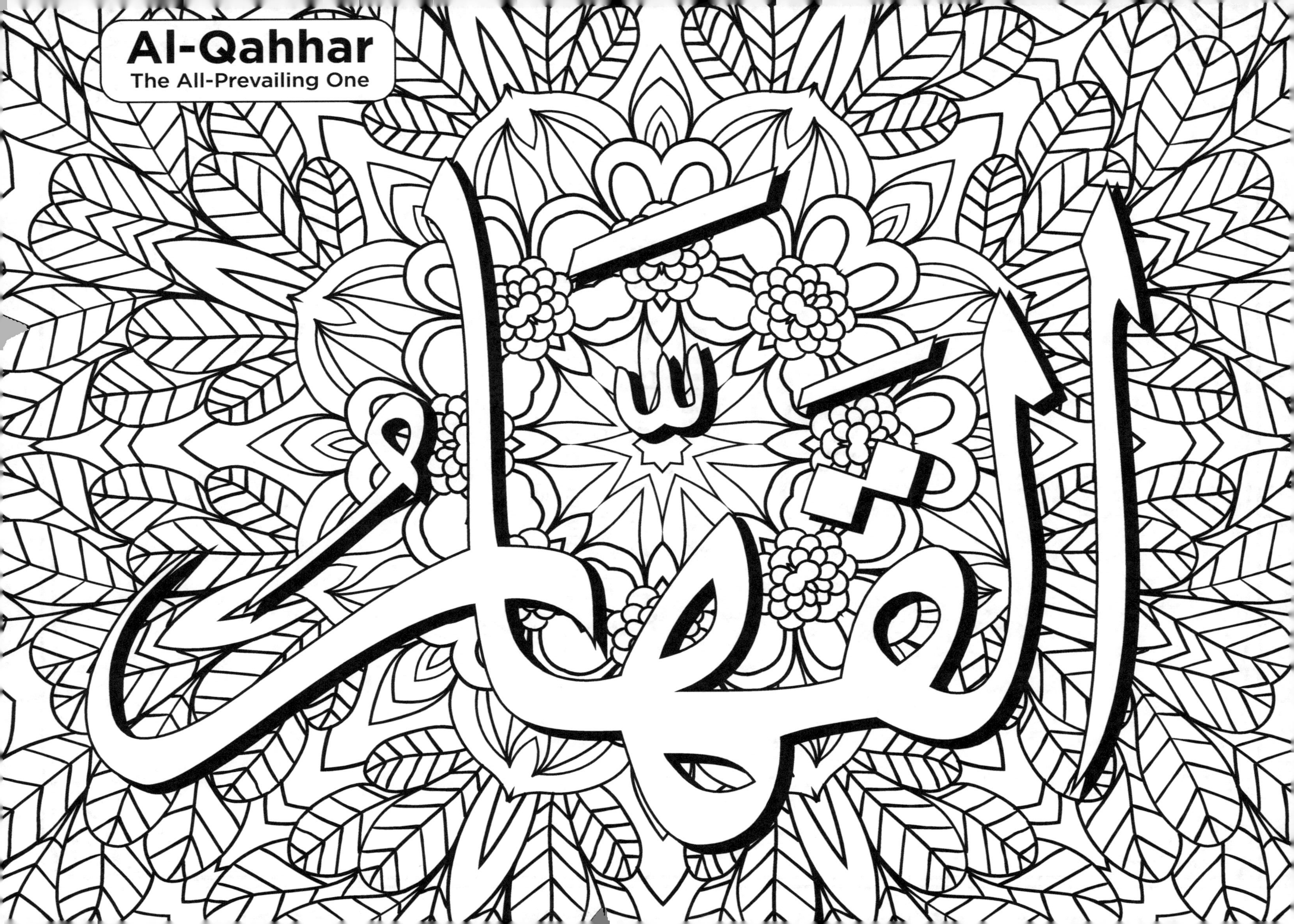
Al-Qahhar
The All-Prevailing One
ٱلْقَهَّارُ

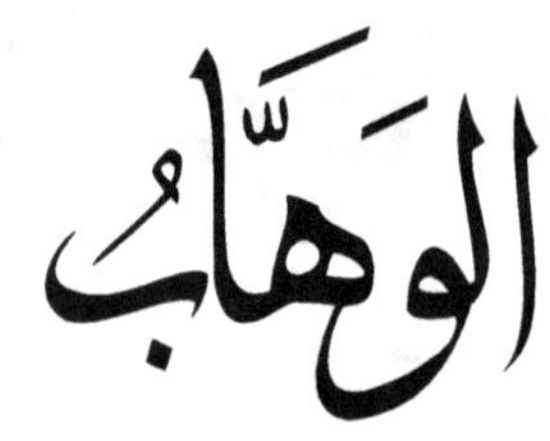

Al-Wahhab

The Supreme Bestower

The One who is Generous
in giving plenty without
any return.

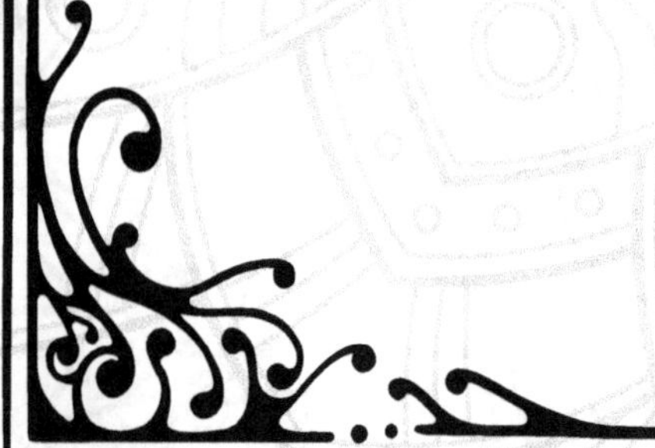

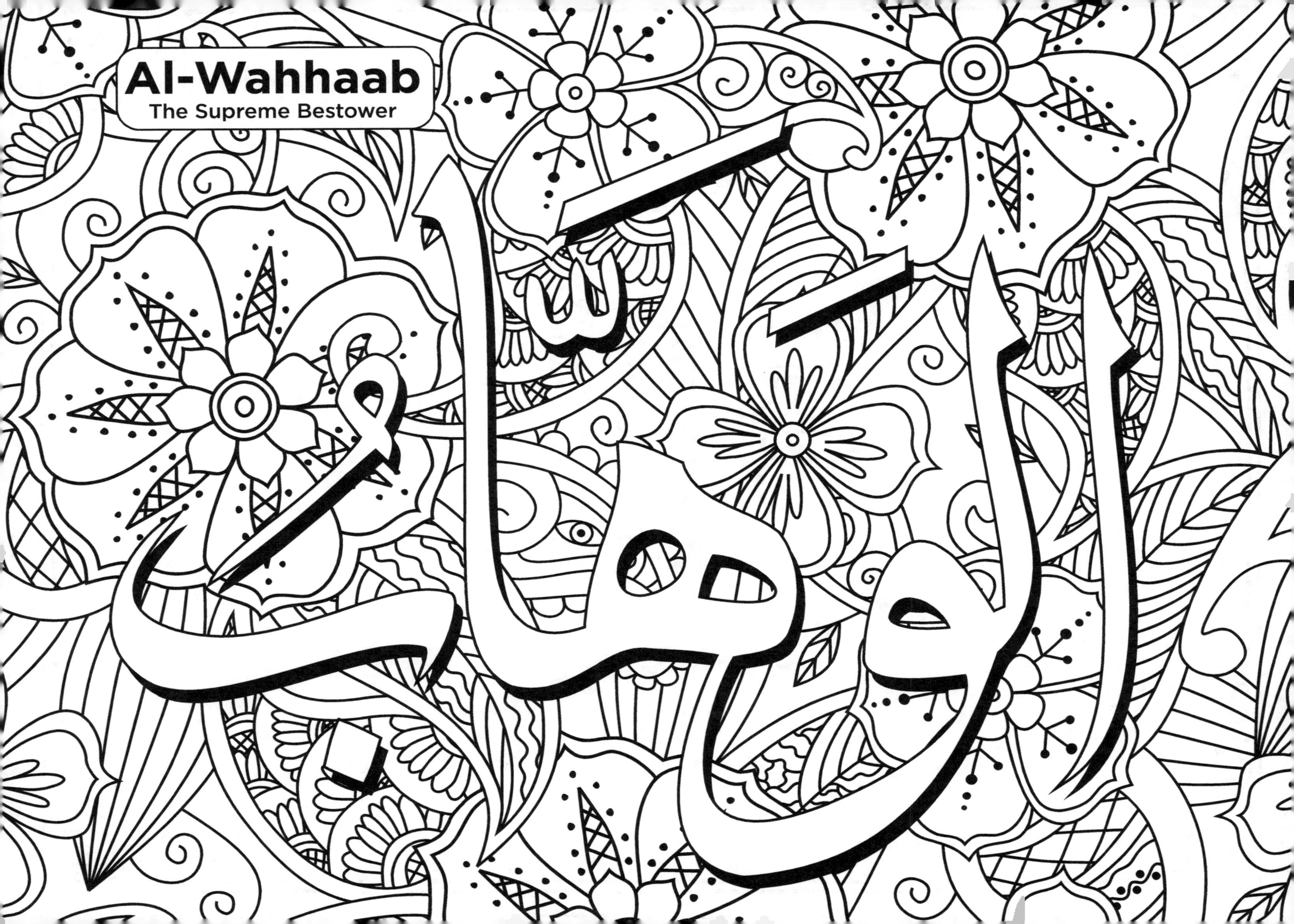
Al-Wahhaab
The Supreme Bestower
الوَهَّاب

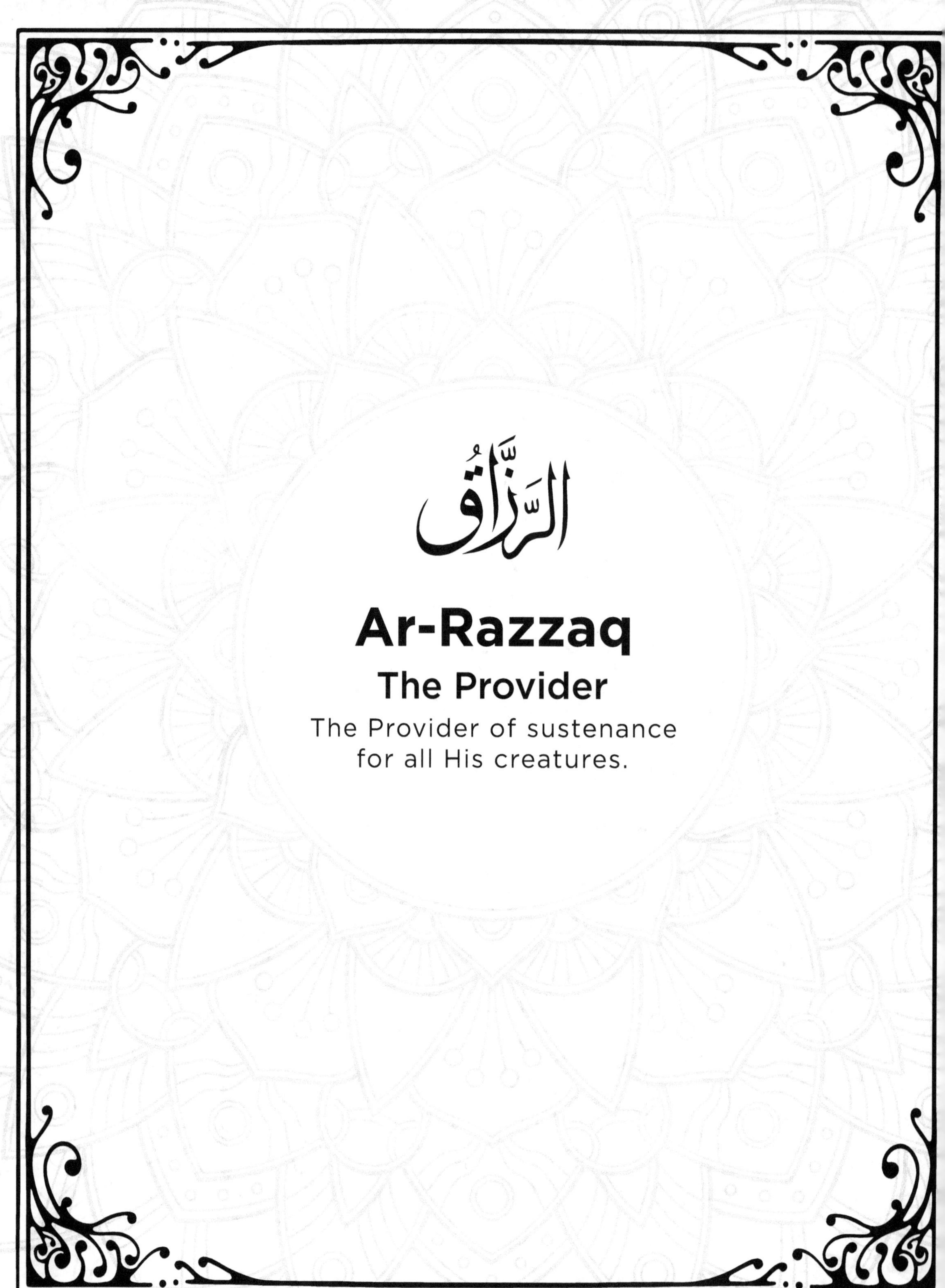

الرَّزَّاقُ

Ar-Razzaq

The Provider

The Provider of sustenance
for all His creatures.

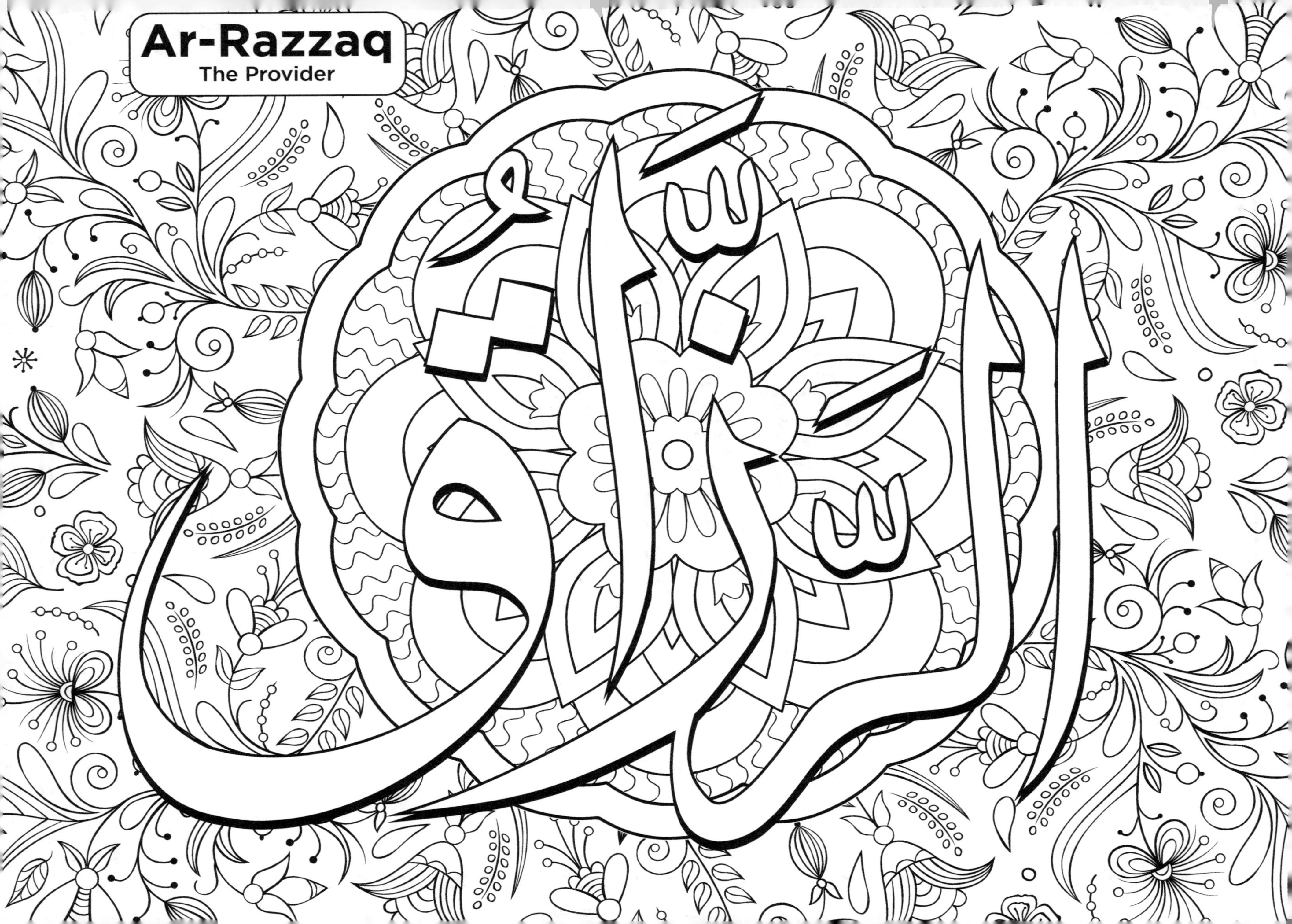
Ar-Razzaq
The Provider
الرَّزَّاقُ

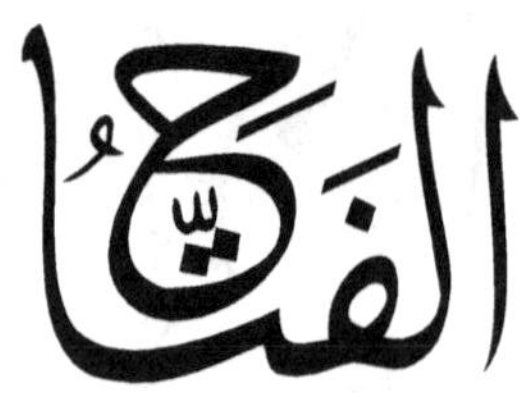

Al-Fattah

The Supreme Solver

The Opener, The Reliever, The Judge, The One who opens for His slaves the closed worldly and religious matters.

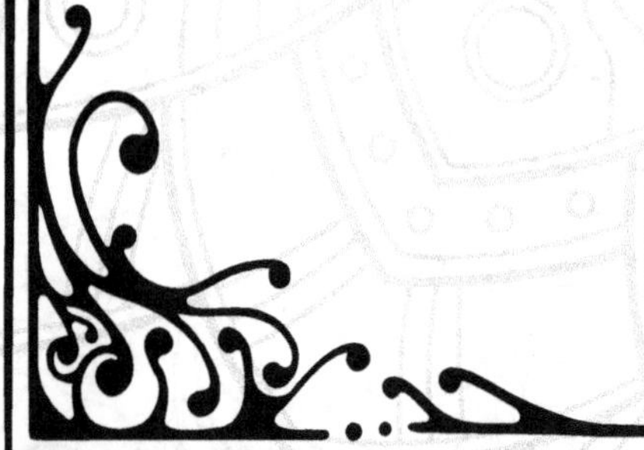

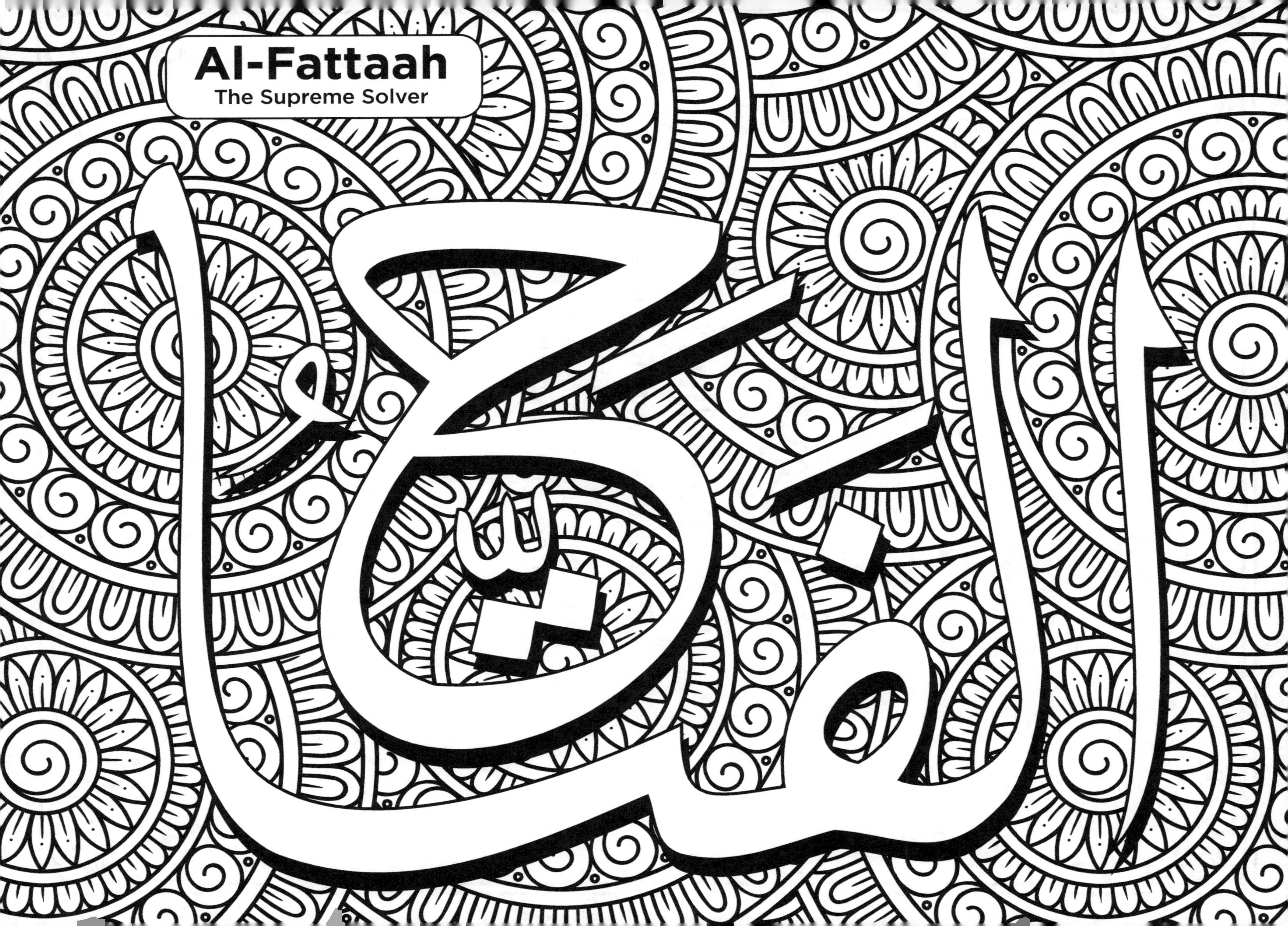
Al-Fattaah
The Supreme Solver
الفتّاح

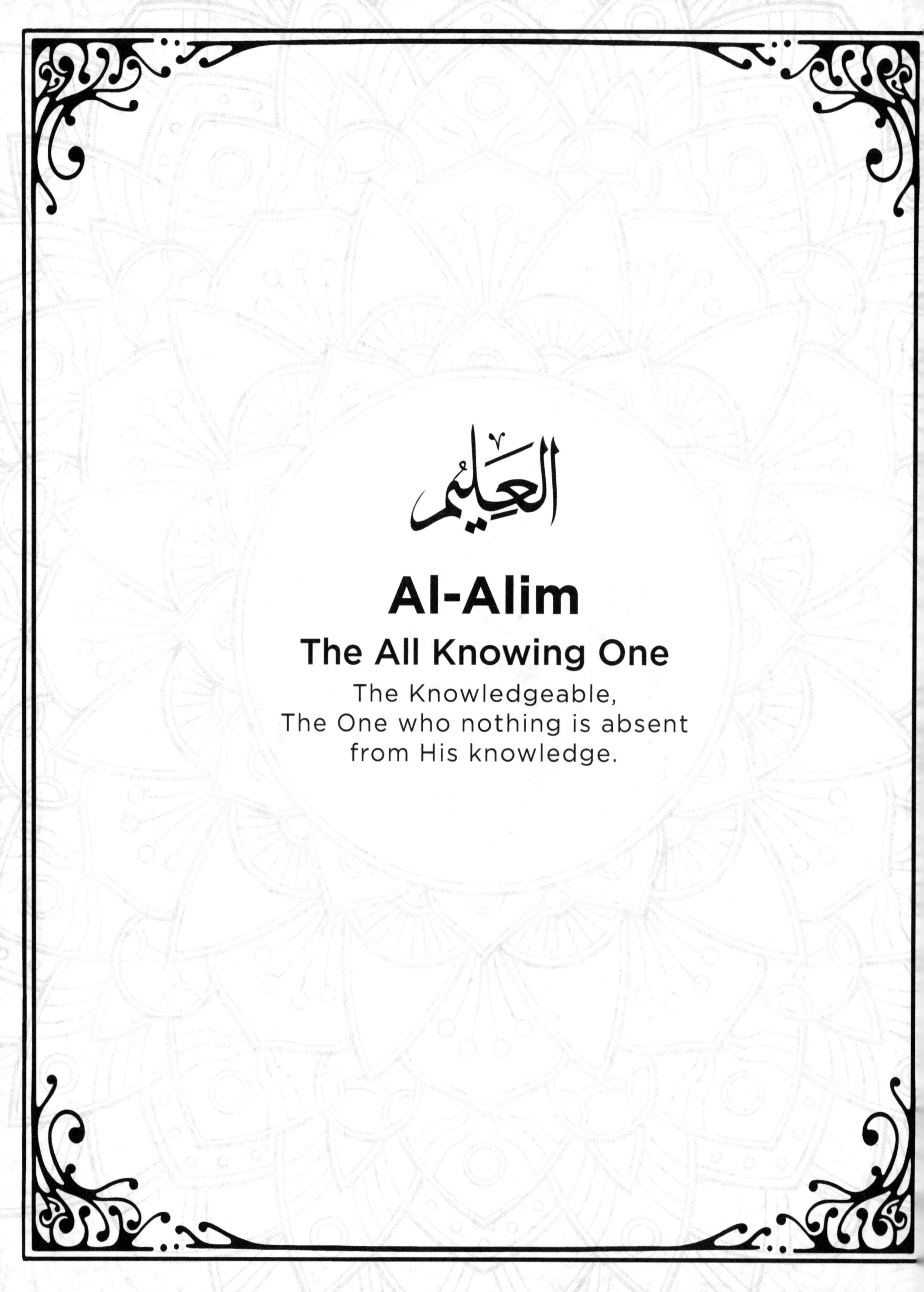

Al-Alim

The All Knowing One

The Knowledgeable,
The One who nothing is absent
from His knowledge.

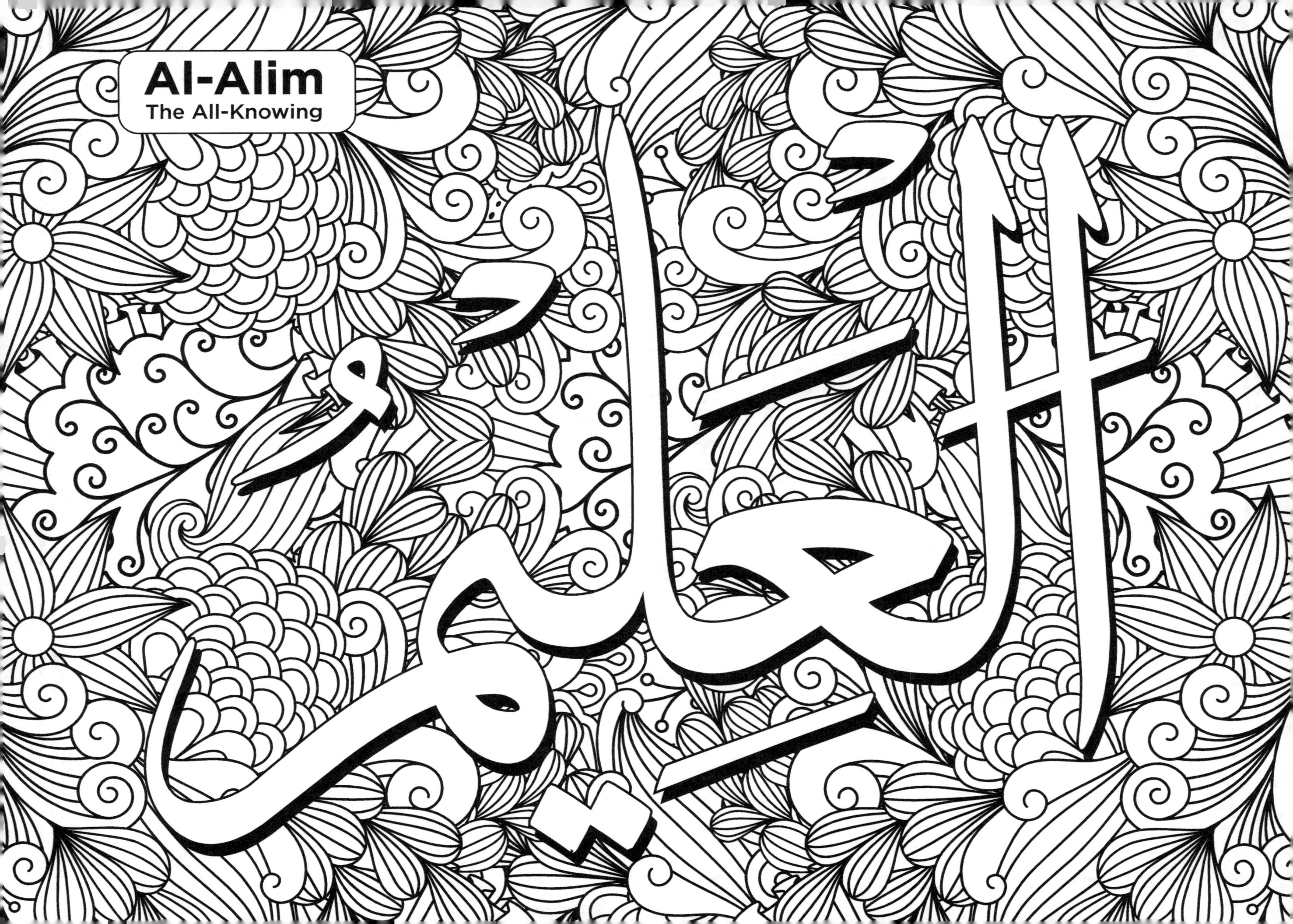
Al-Alim
The All-Knowing
ٱلْعَلِيمُ

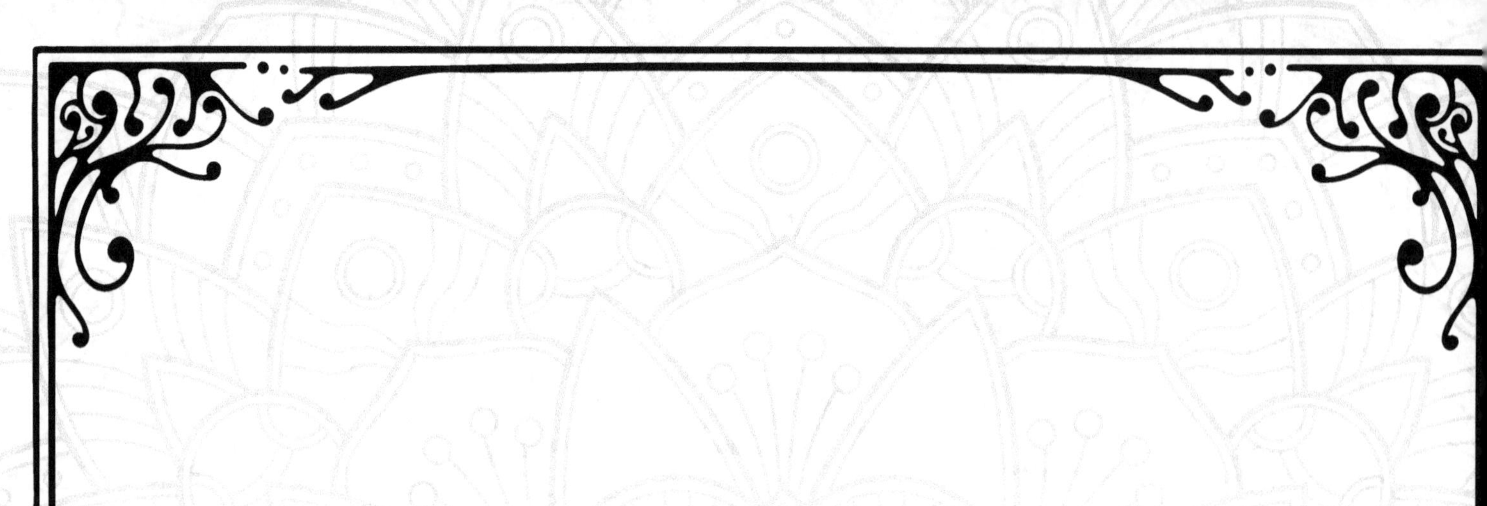

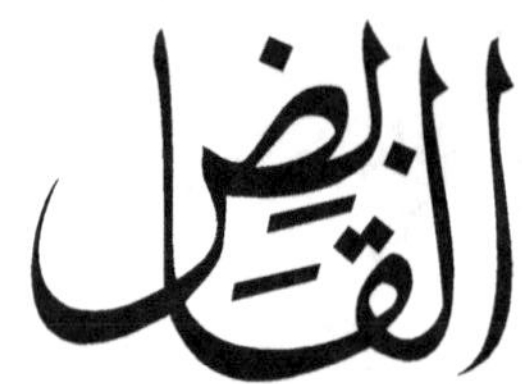

Al-Qaabid

The Restricting One

The Constrictor, The Withholder, The One who constricts the sustenance by His Wisdom.

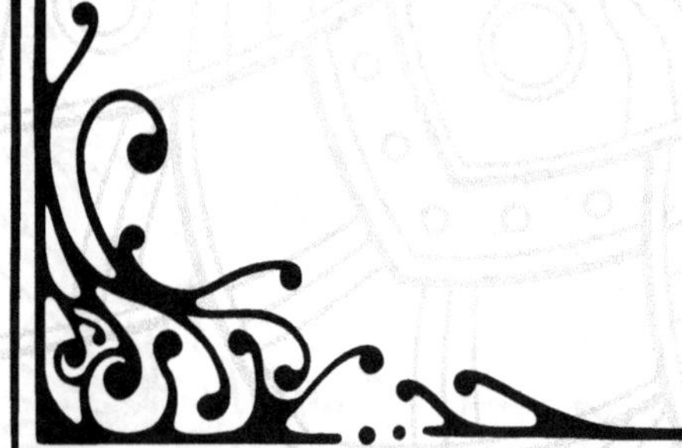

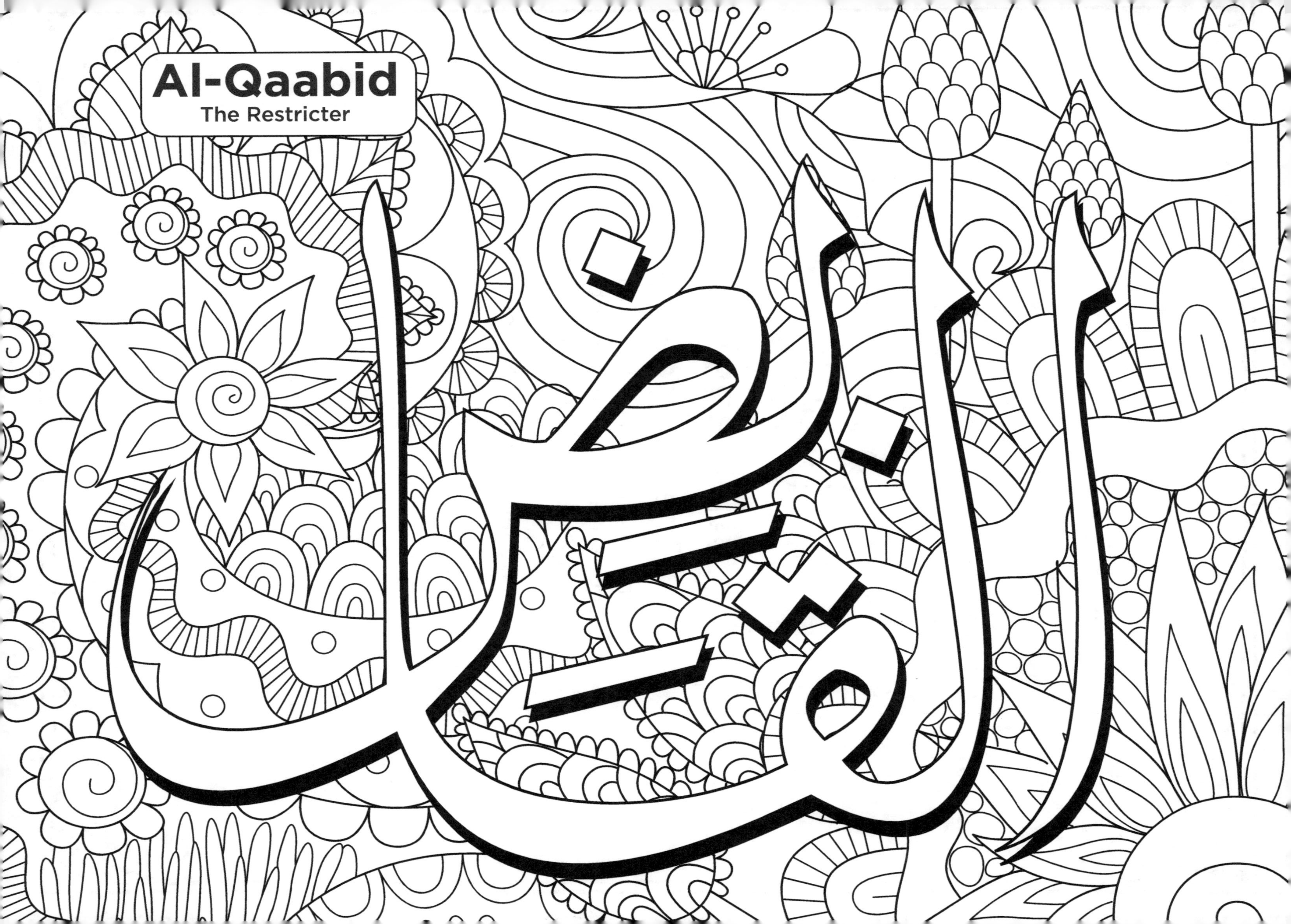
Al-Qaabid
The Restricter
القابض

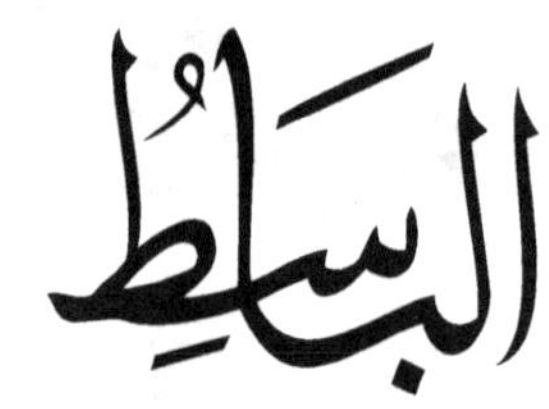

Al-Baasit

The Extender

The Enlarger, The One who constricts the sustenance by His wisdom and expands and widens it with His Generosity and Mercy.

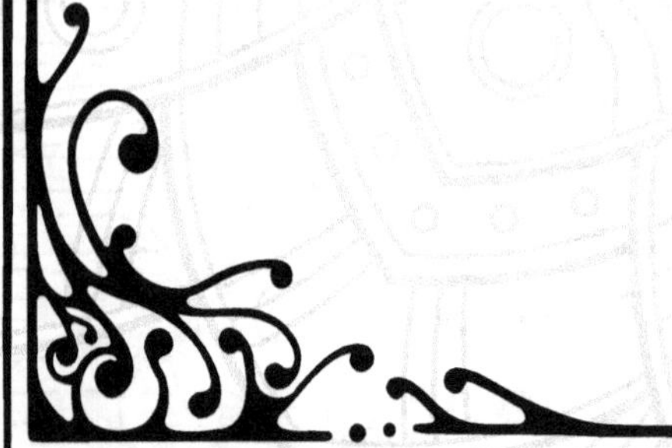

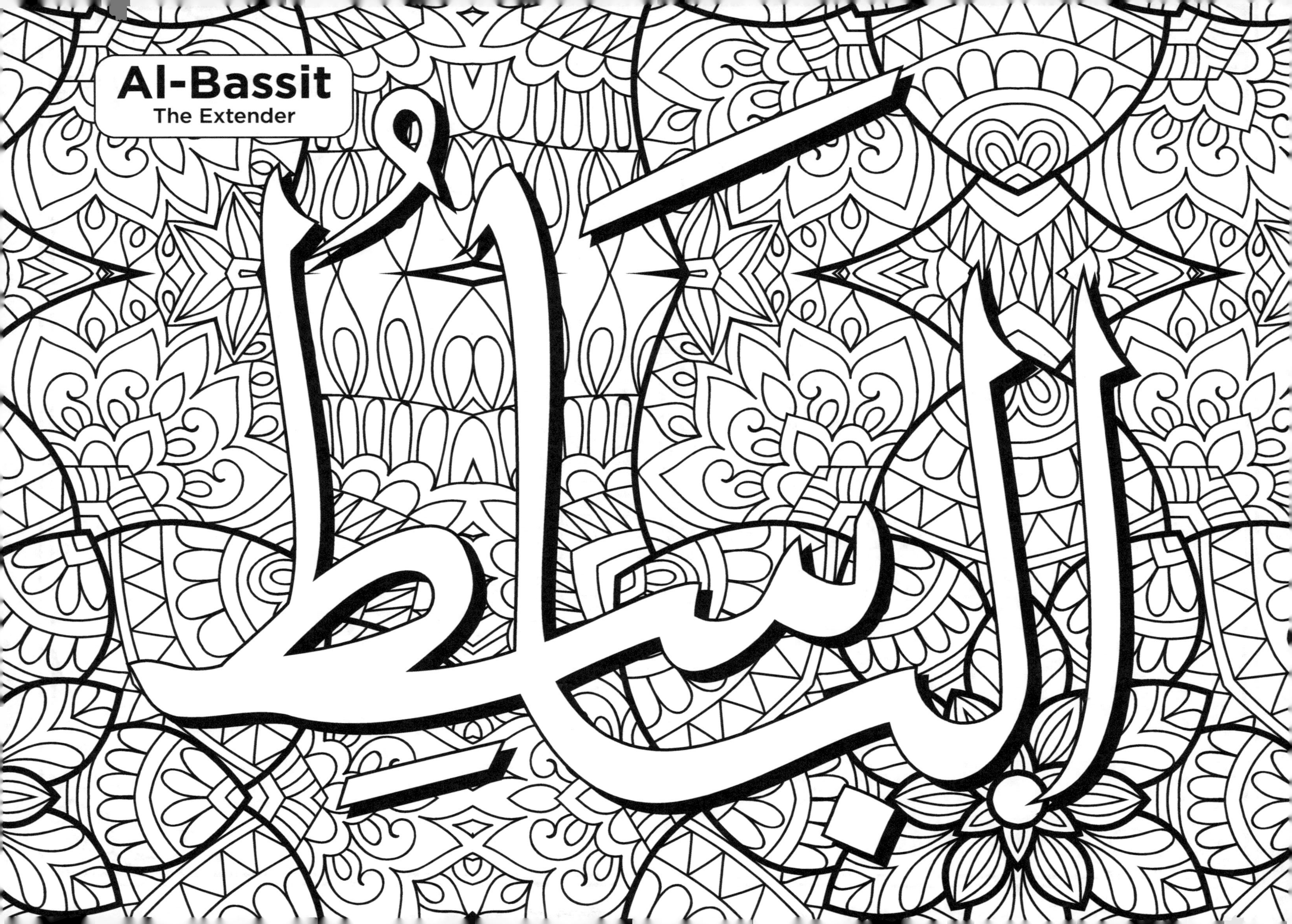
Al-Bassit
The Extender
البَسِطُ

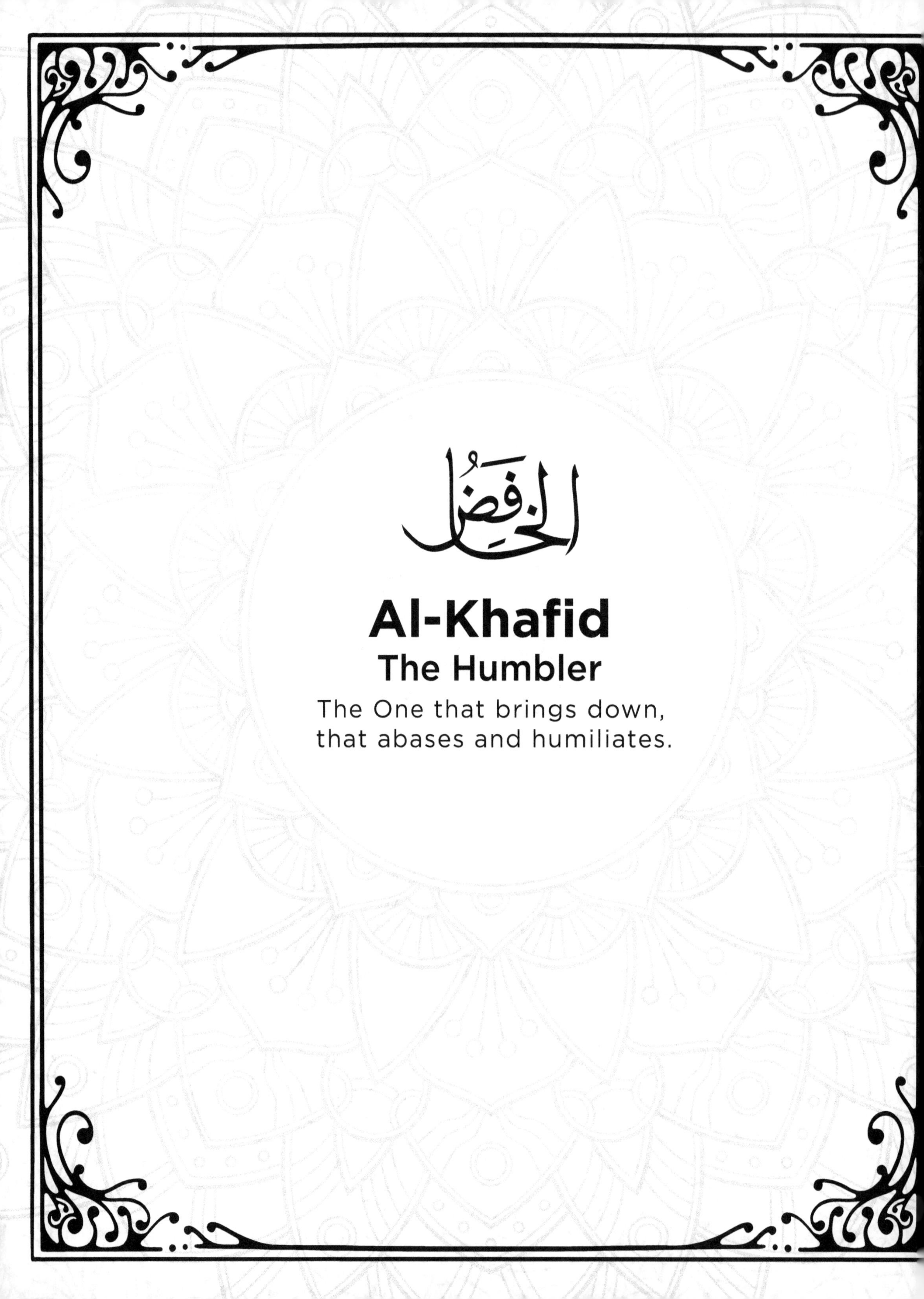

الخَافِضُ

Al-Khafid

The Humbler

The One that brings down, that abases and humiliates.

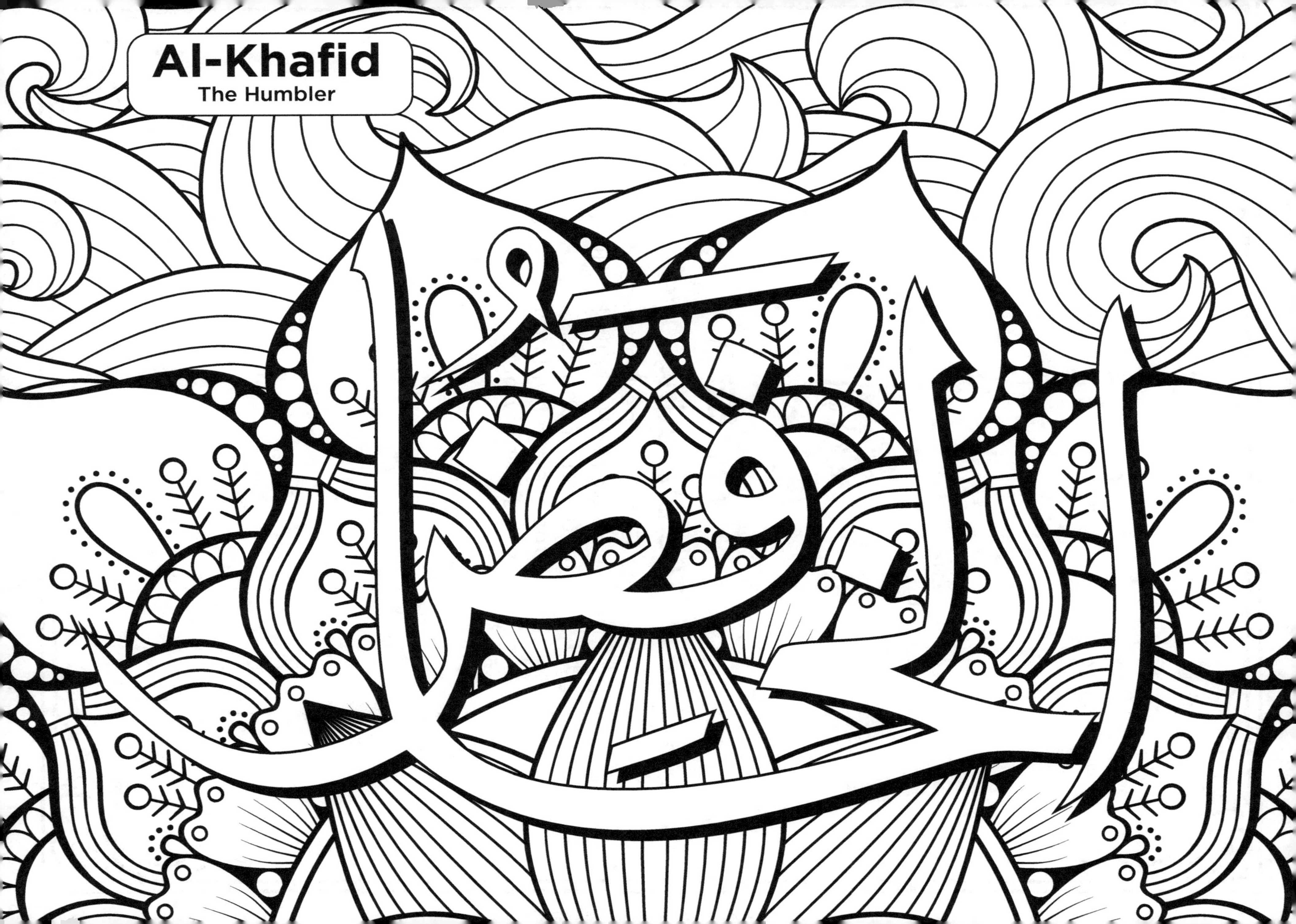
Al-Khafid
The Humbler

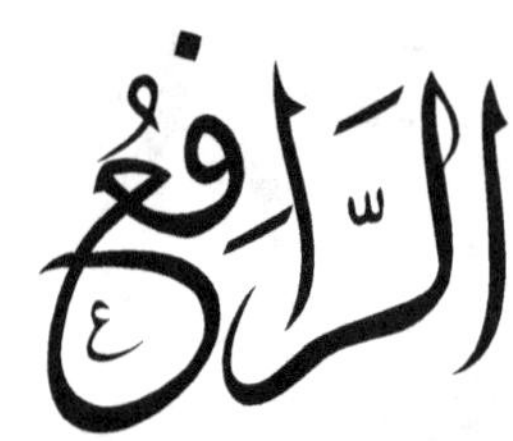

Ar-Raafi’

The Elevating One

The Exalter, The One who lowers whoever He wills by His Destruction and raises whoever He wills by His Endowment.

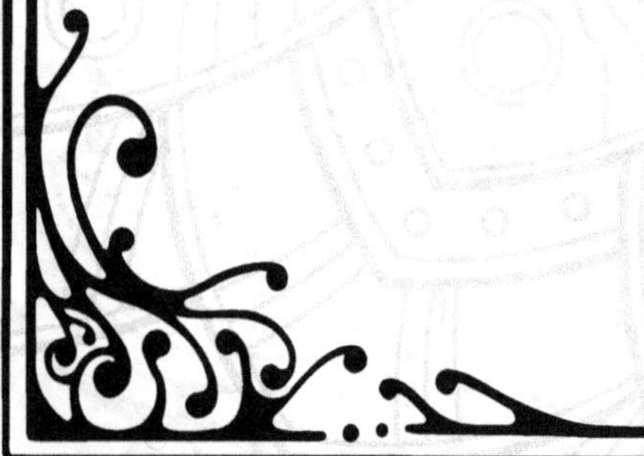

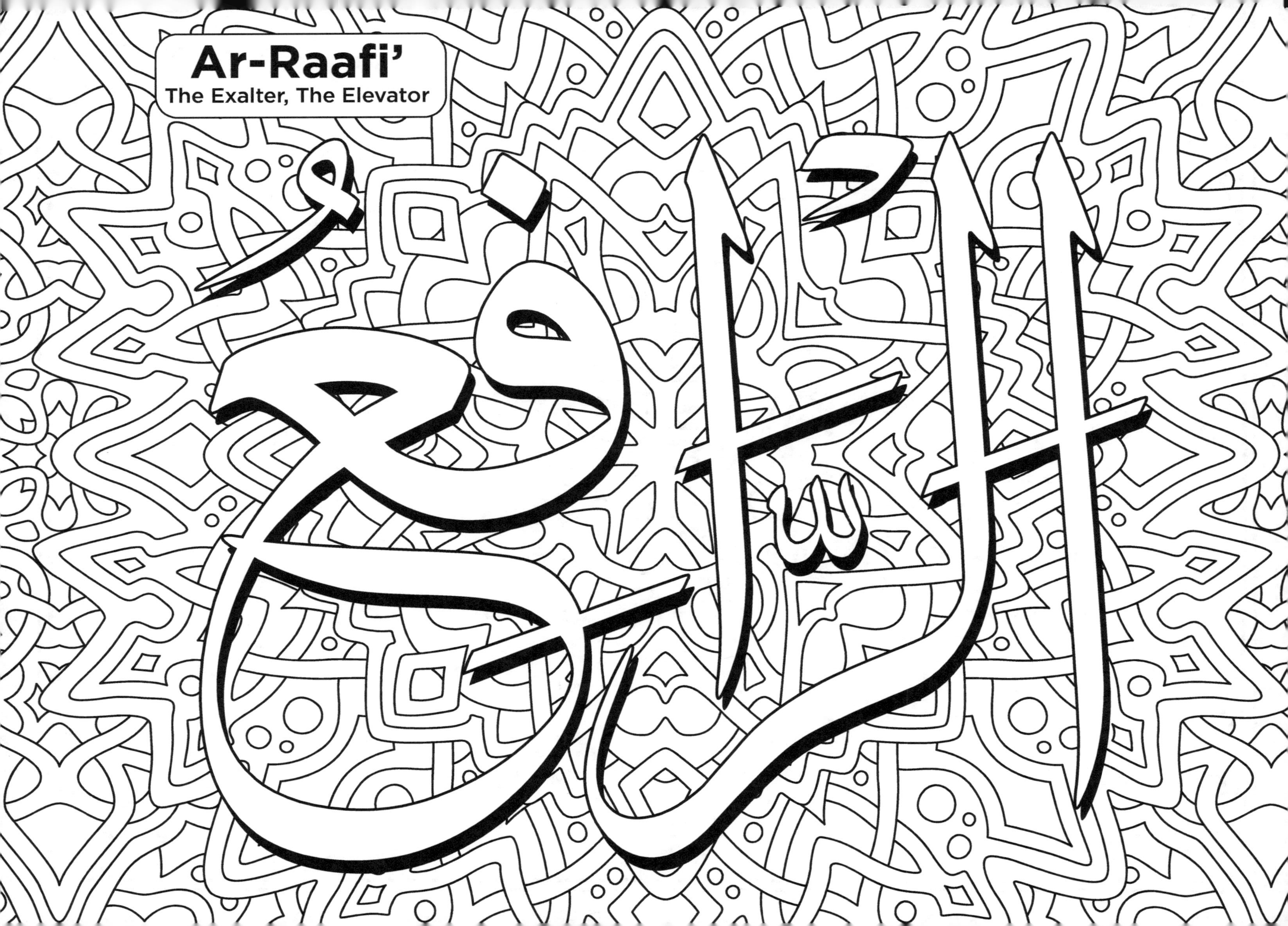
Ar-Raafi’
The Exalter, The Elevator
الرَّافِعُ

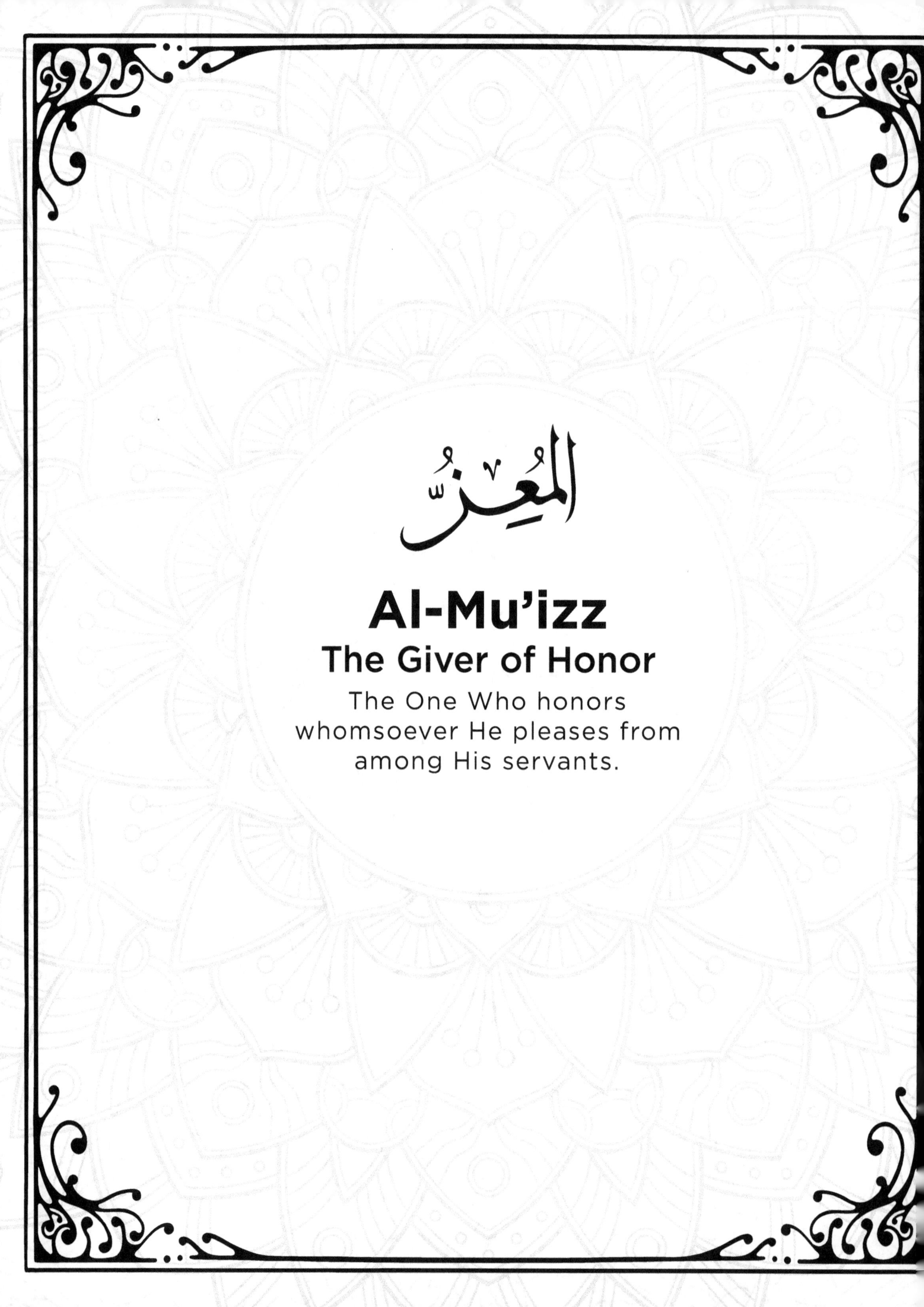

Al-Mu'izz

The Giver of Honor

The One Who honors whomsoever He pleases from among His servants.

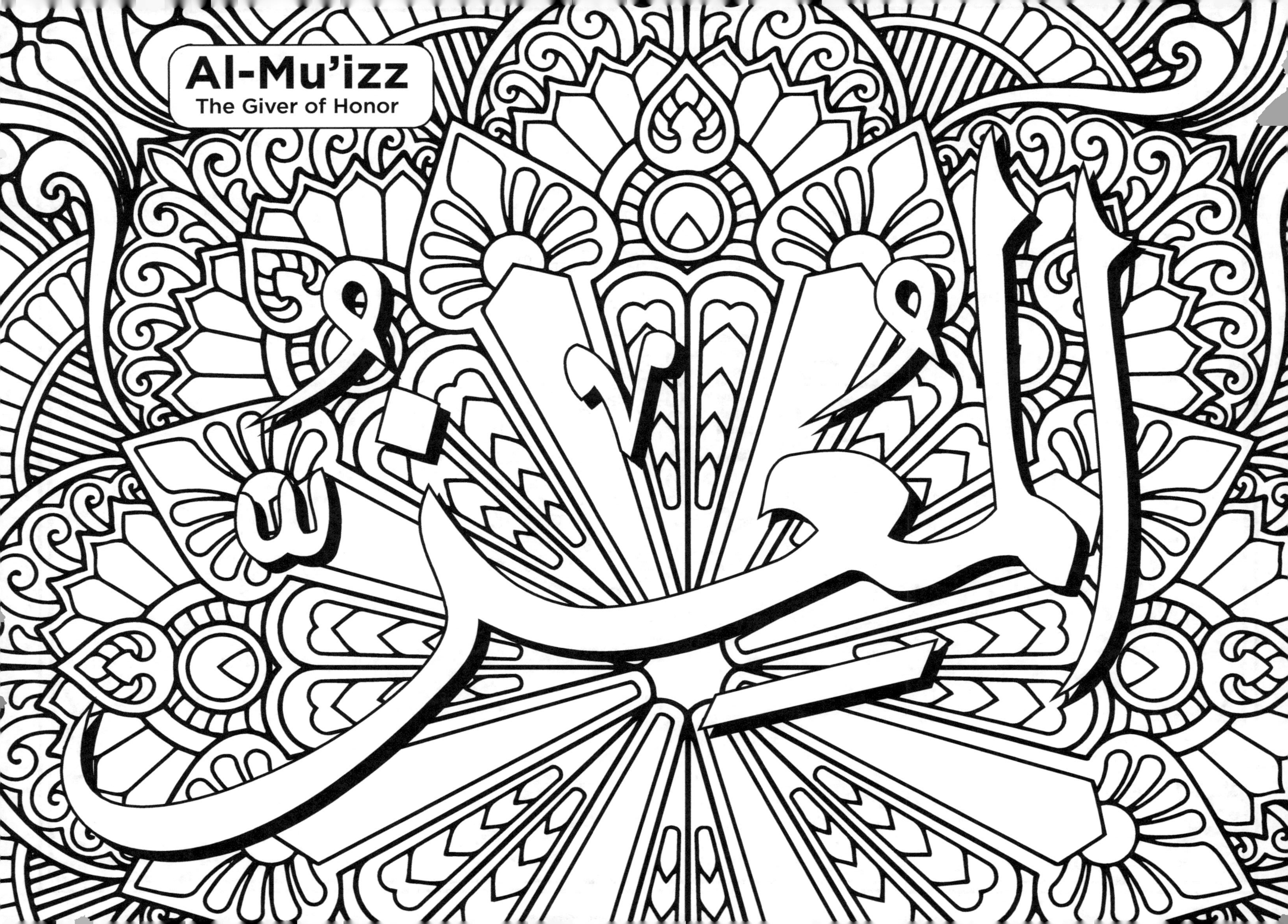
Al-Mu'izz
The Giver of Honor

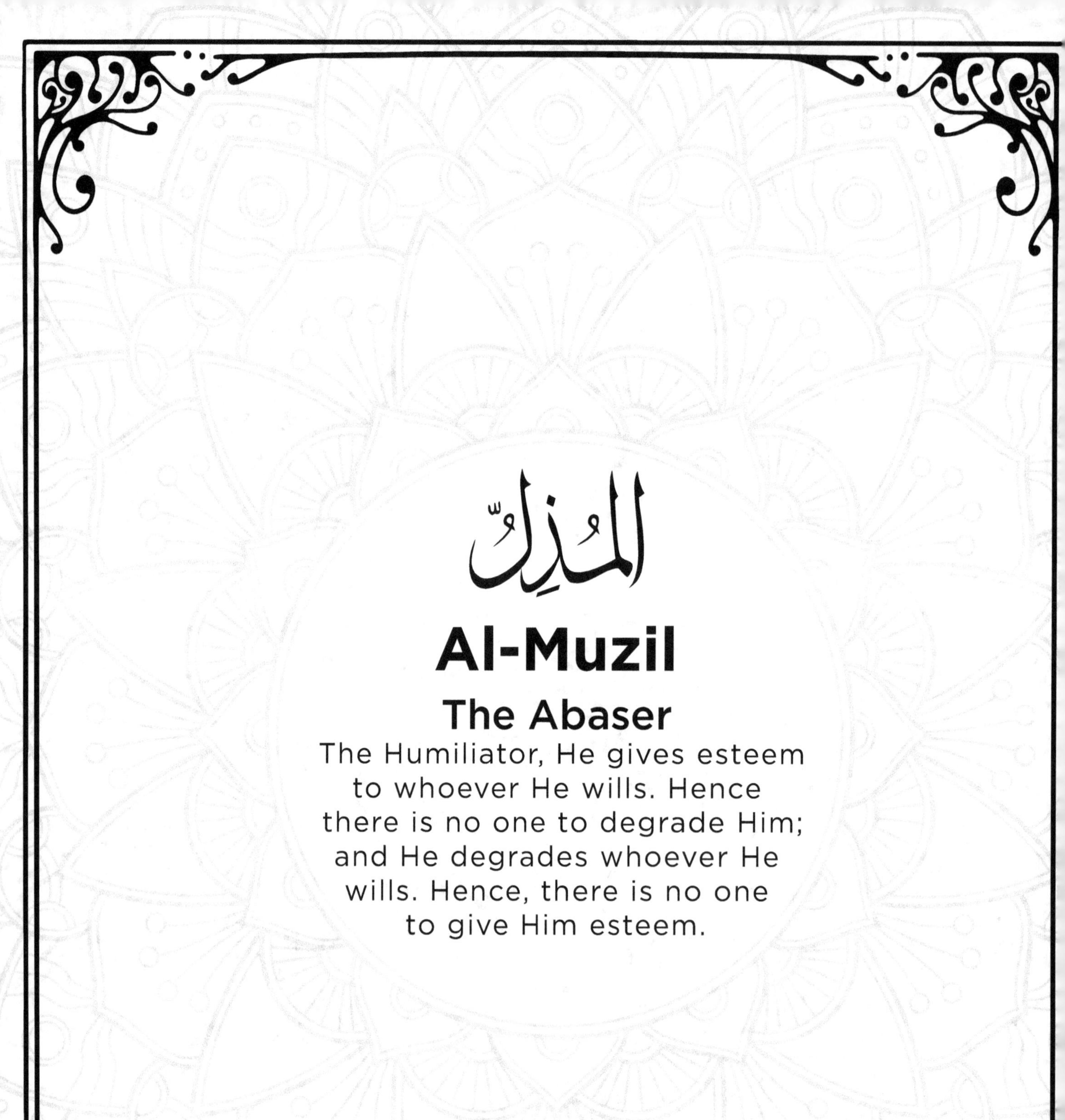

المذل

Al-Muzil

The Abaser

The Humiliator, He gives esteem to whoever He wills. Hence there is no one to degrade Him; and He degrades whoever He wills. Hence, there is no one to give Him esteem.

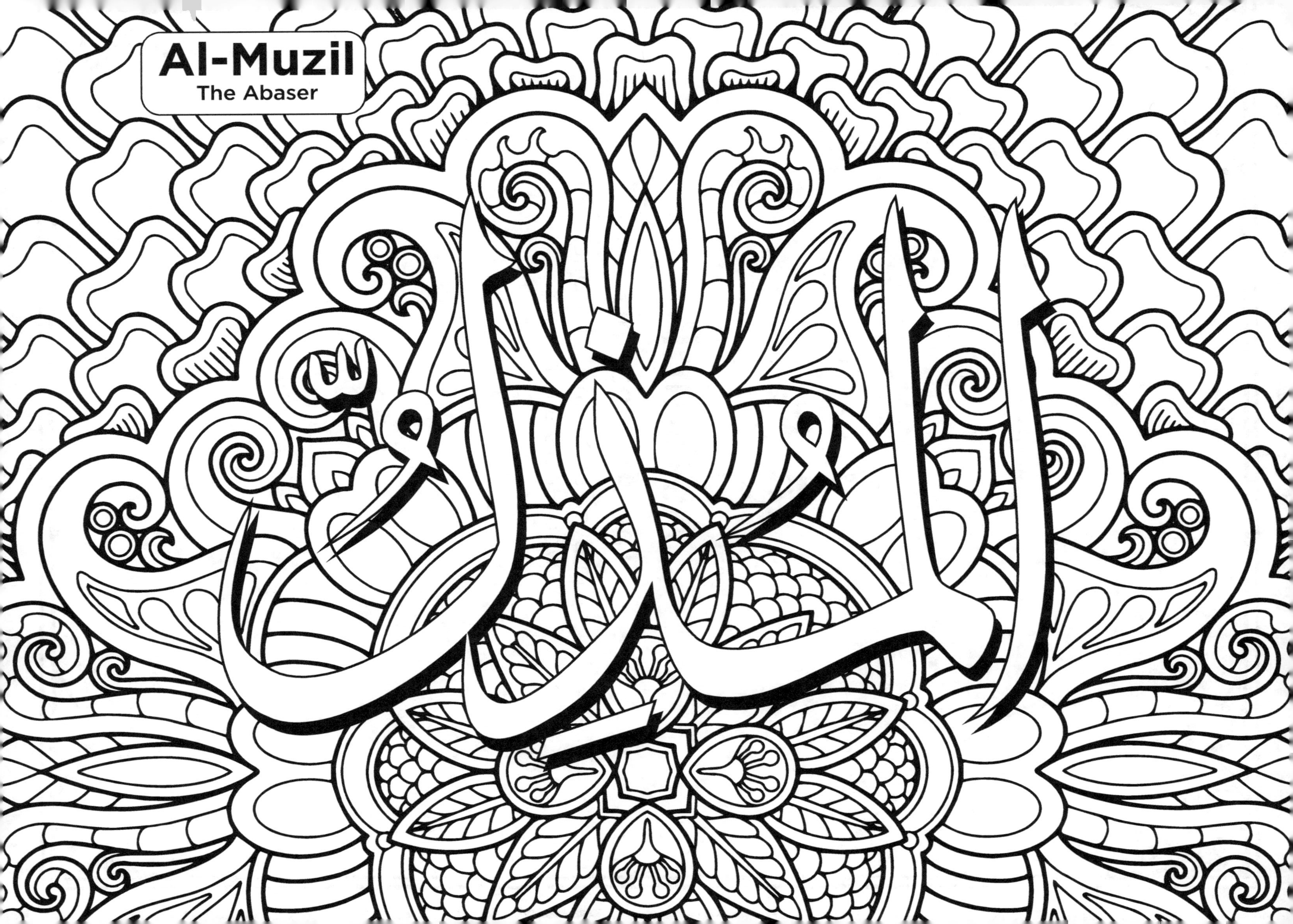
Al-Muzil
The Abaser

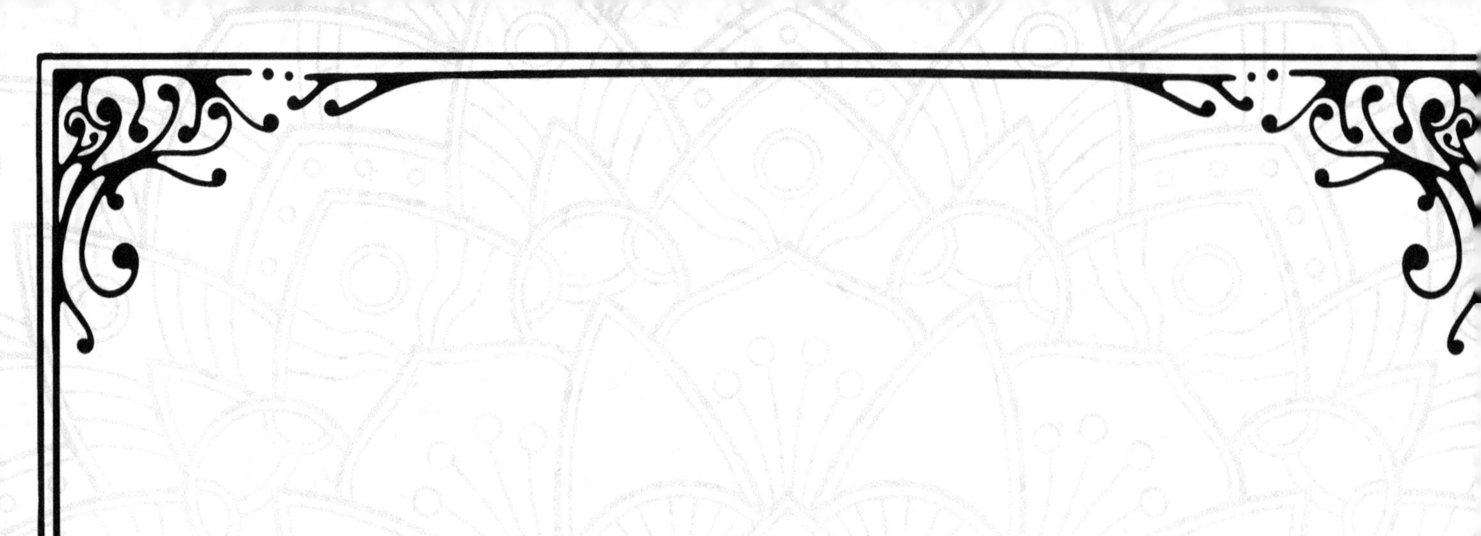

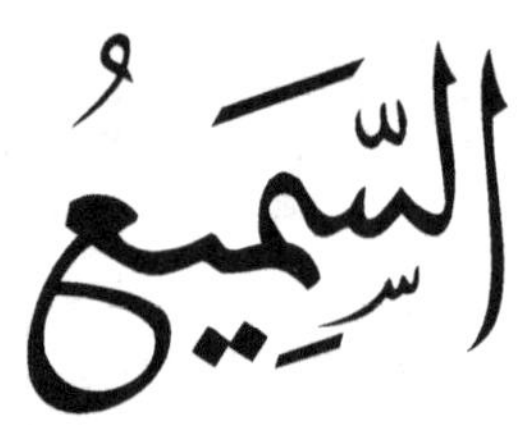

As-Sami'

The All-Hearing

The Ever-Listening. The One who Hears all things.

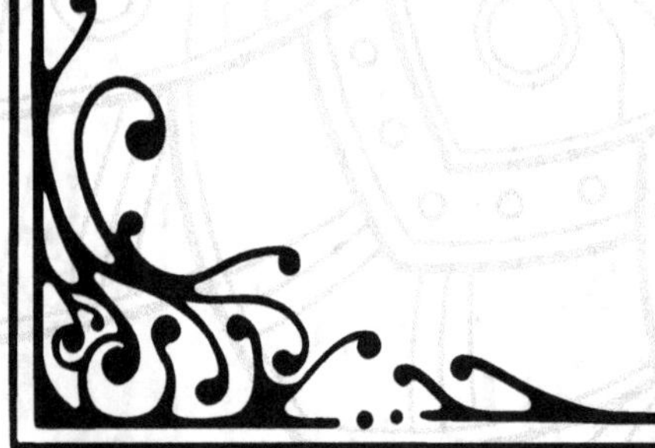

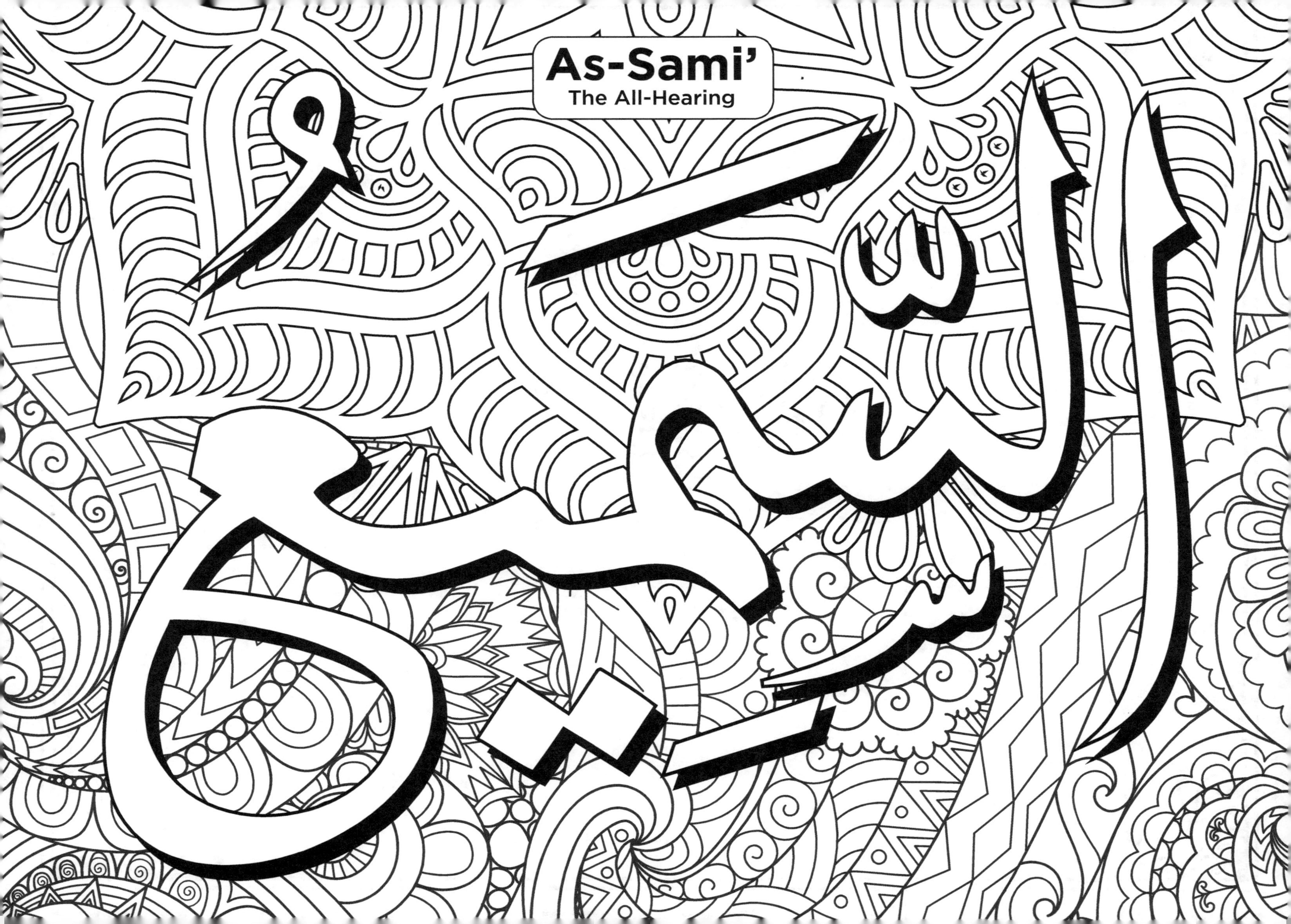
As-Sami'
The All-Hearing
السميع

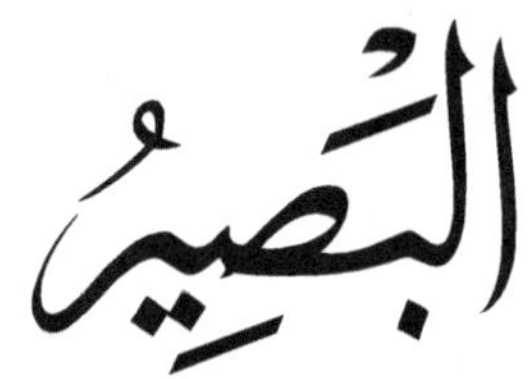

Al-Baseer

The All-Seeing

The All-Noticing.
The One who sees all things
open or hidden.

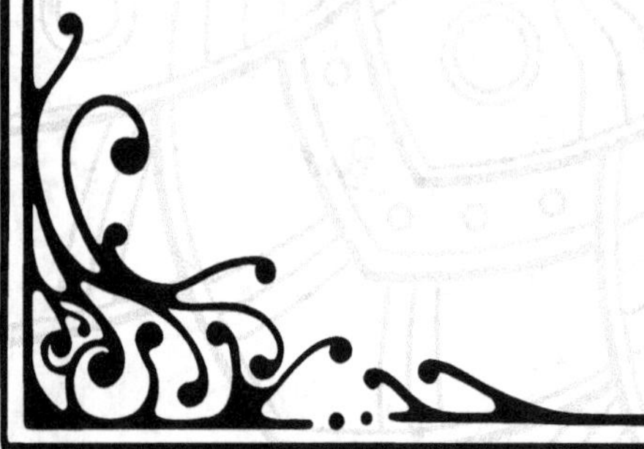

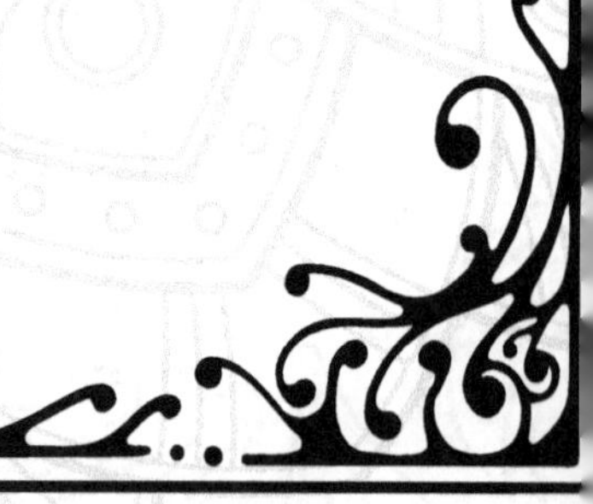

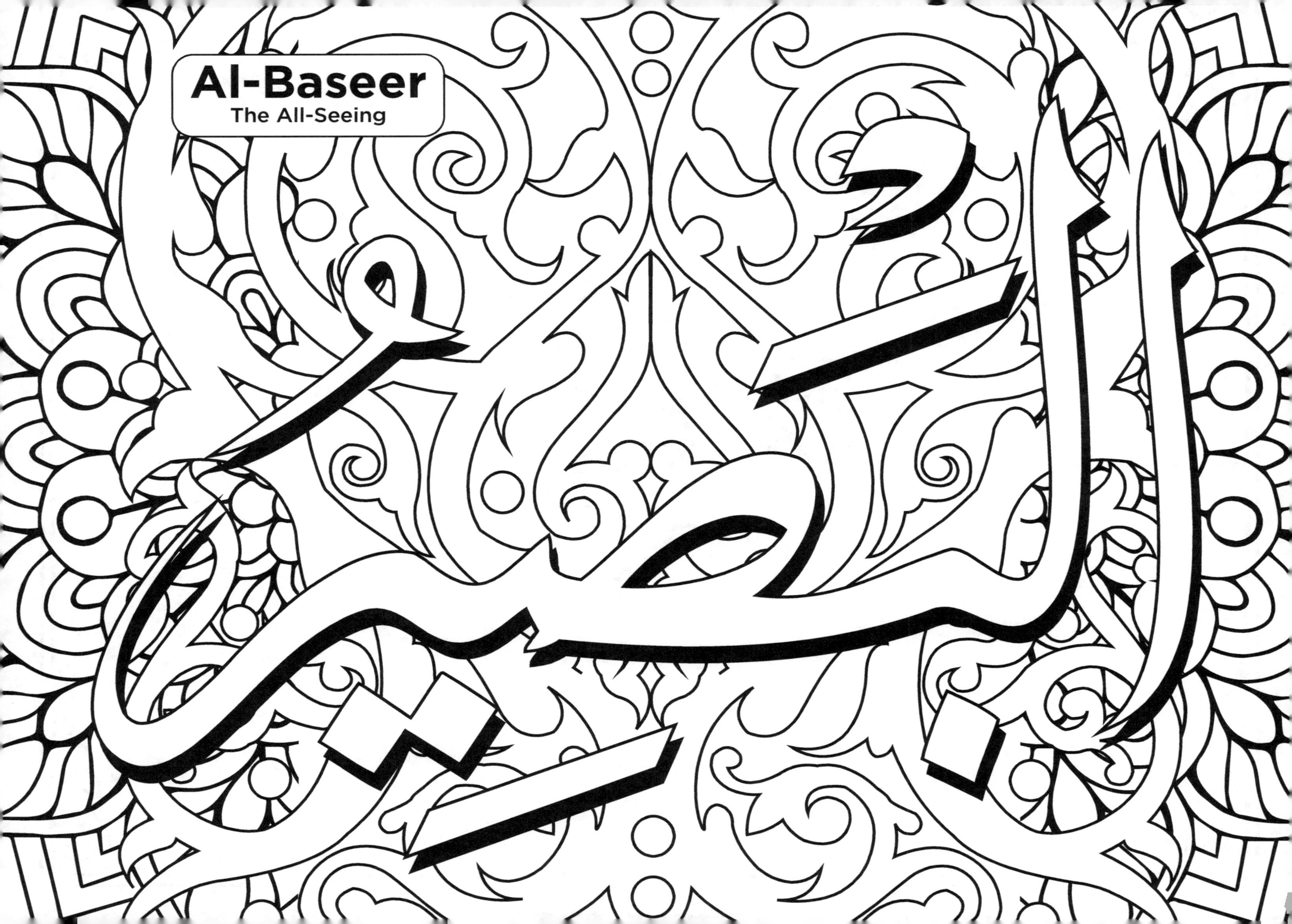
Al-Baseer
The All-Seeing
البصير

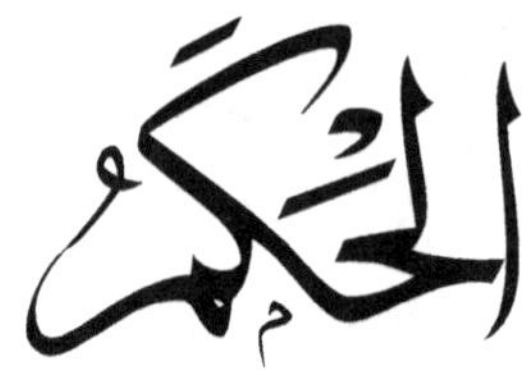

Al-Hakim

The Impartial Judge

The Judge, Ruler and His Judgment is His Word.

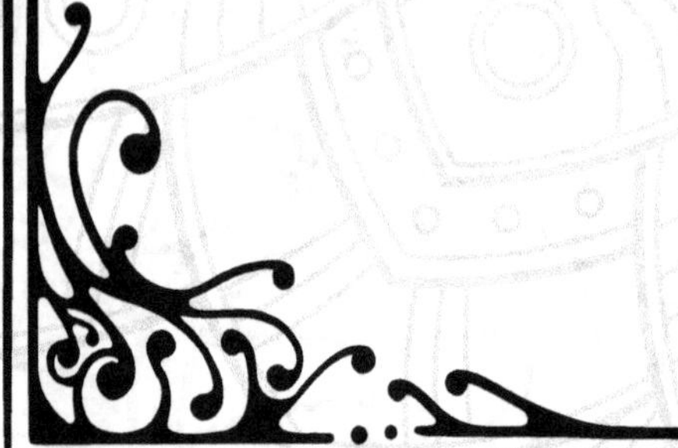

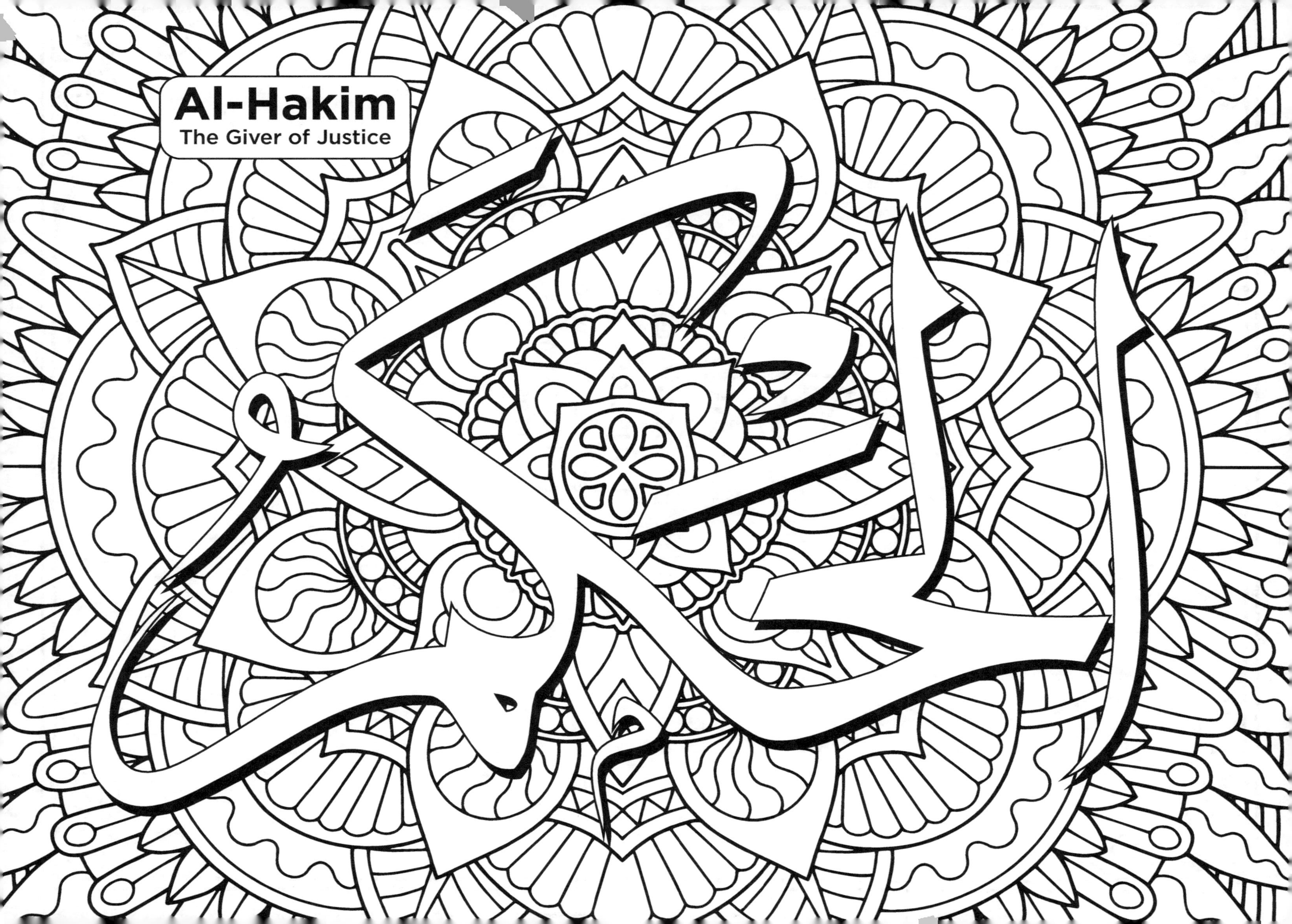
Al-Hakim
The Giver of Justice
الحكيم

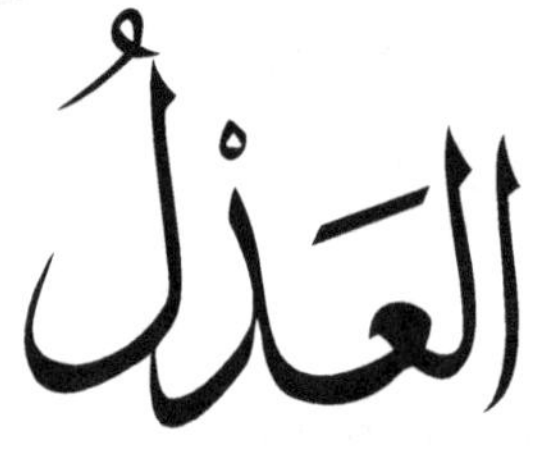

Al-Adl

The Embodiment of Justice

The Just. The One who is entitled to do what He does.

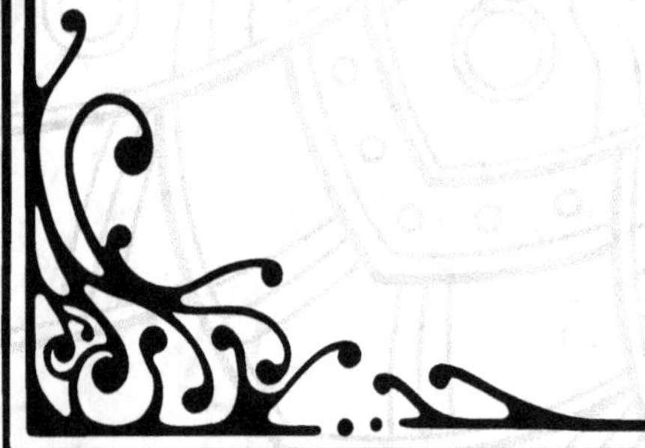

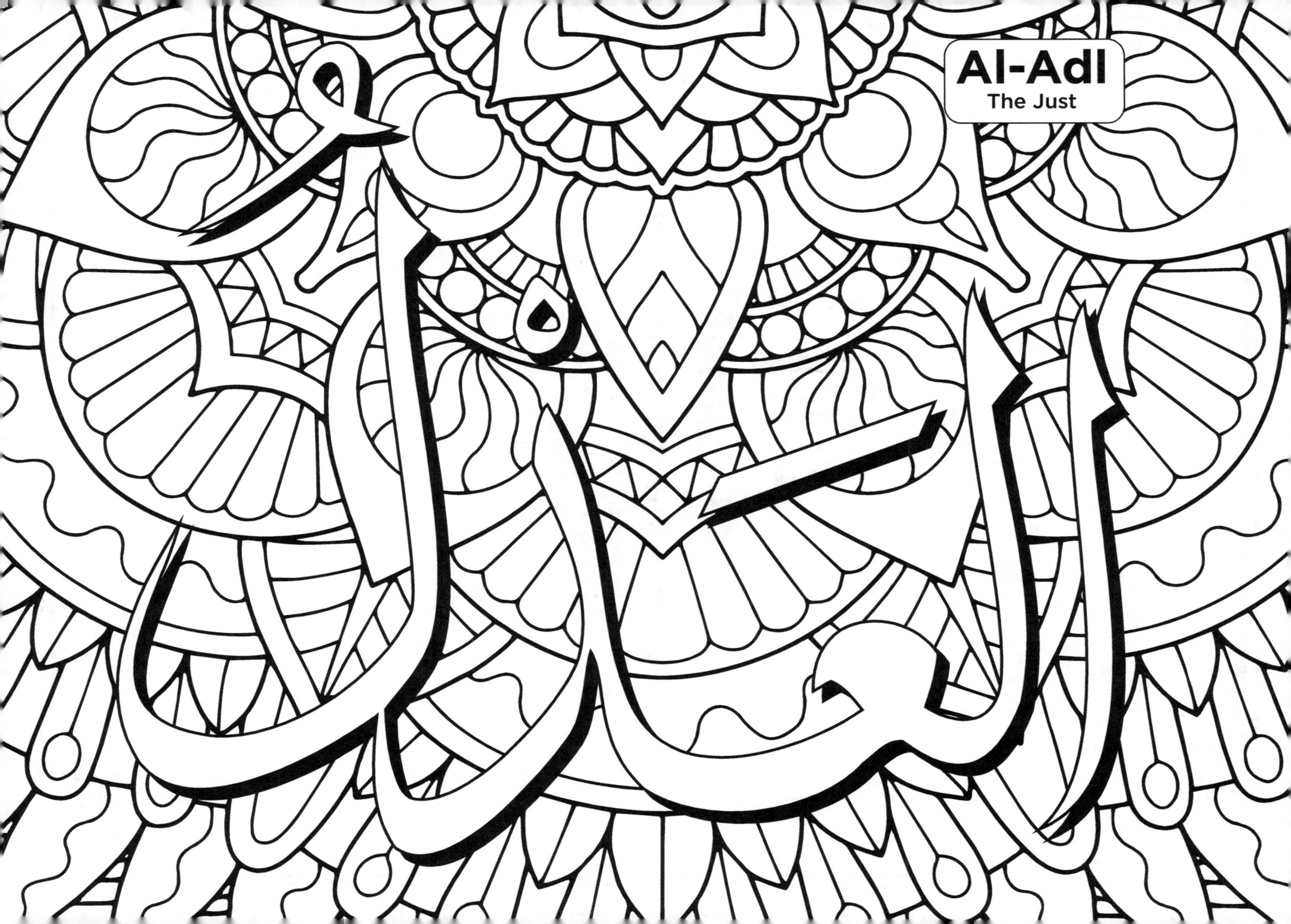
Al-Adl
The Just
العدل

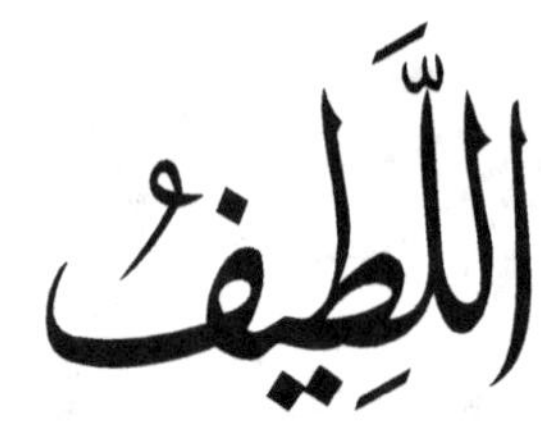

Al-Lateef

The Knower of Subtleties

The Subtle One, The Gracious,
The One who is kind to His
slaves and endows
upon them.

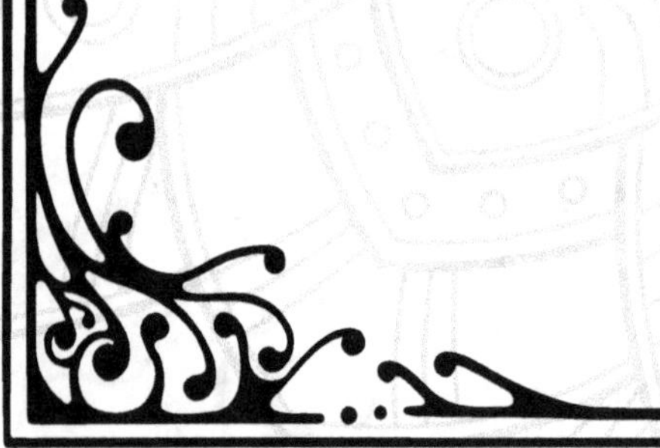

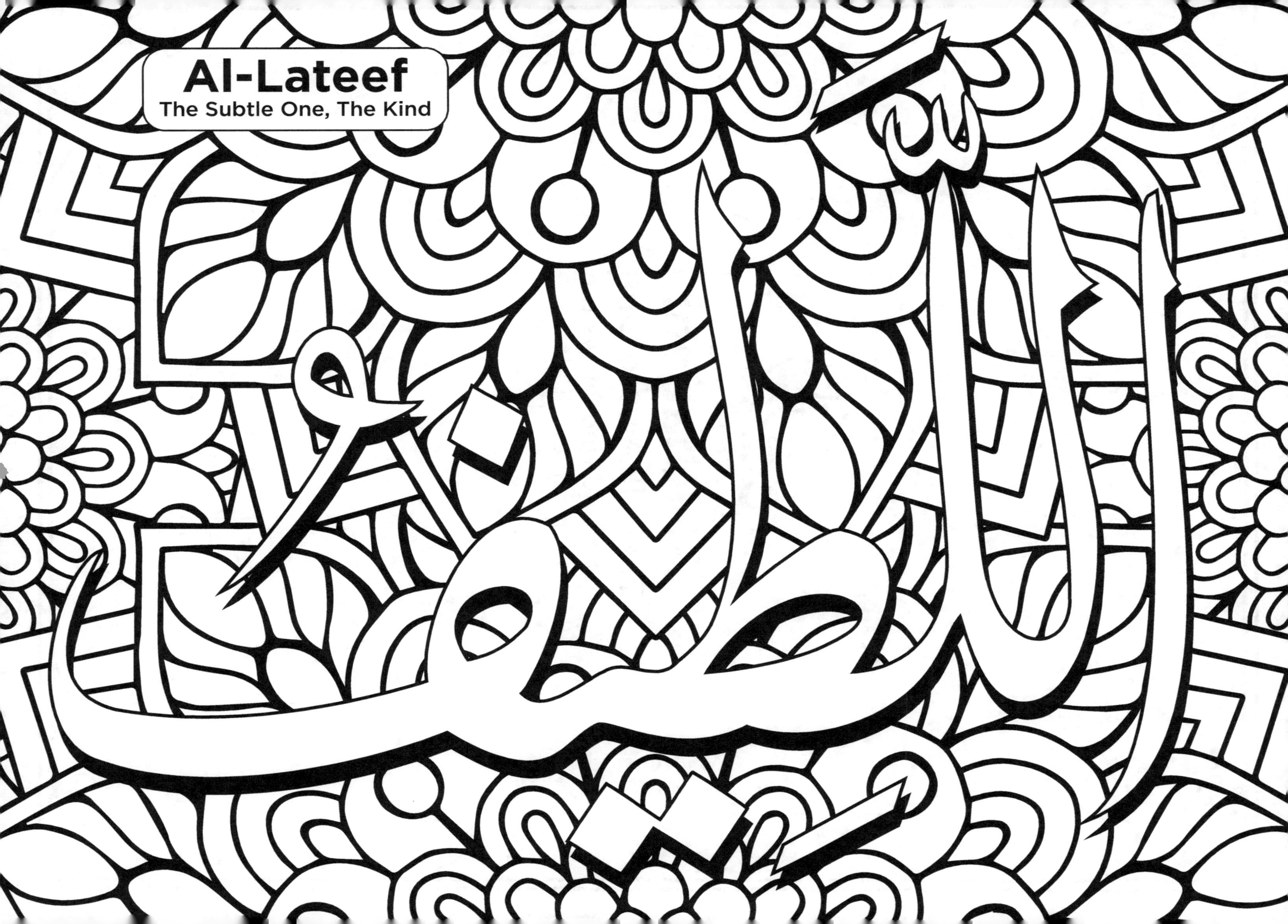
Al-Lateef
The Subtle One, The Kind
اللطيف

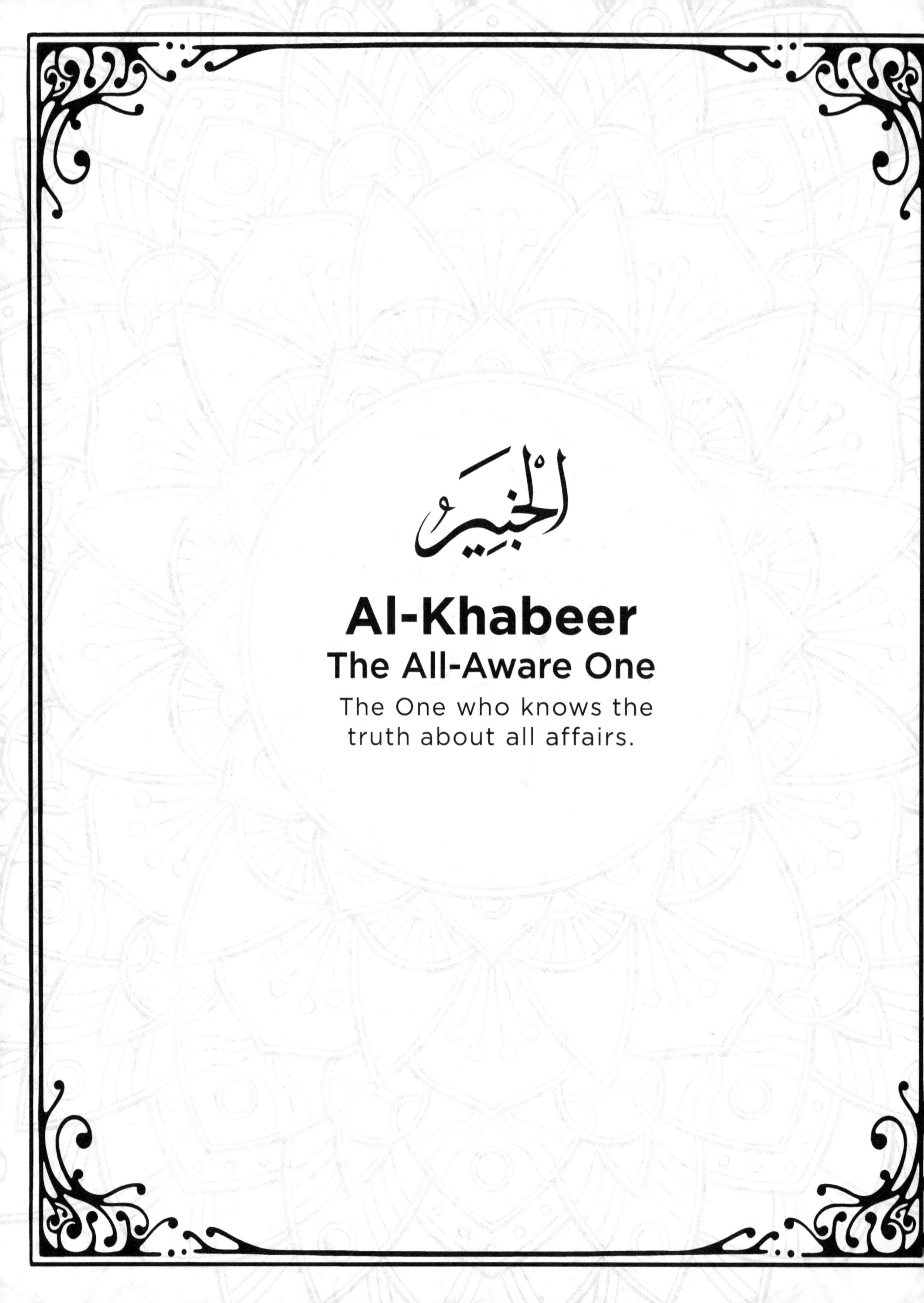

الْخَبِيرُ

Al-Khabeer

The All-Aware One

The One who knows the truth about all affairs.

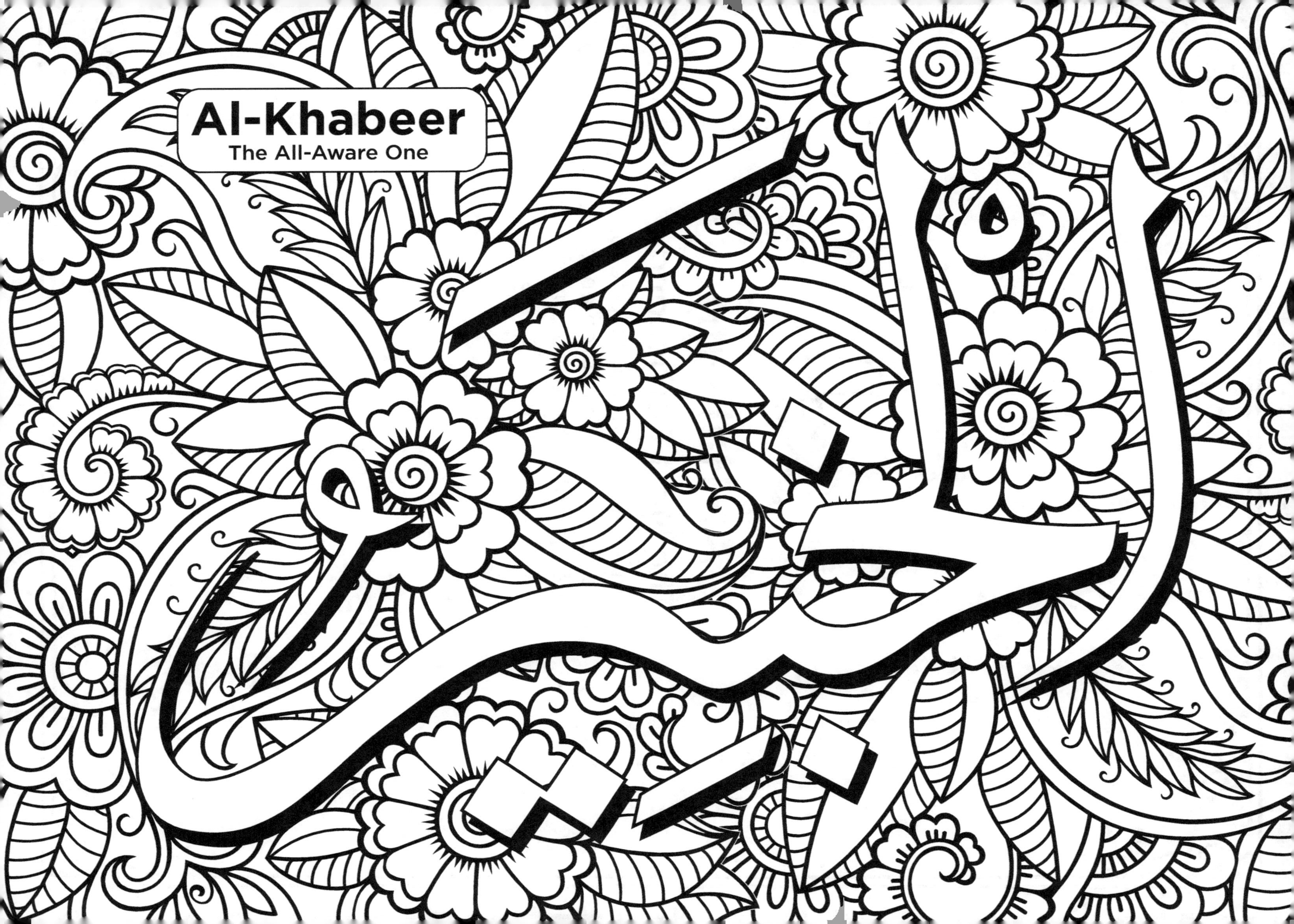
الخبير
Al-Khabeer
The All-Aware One

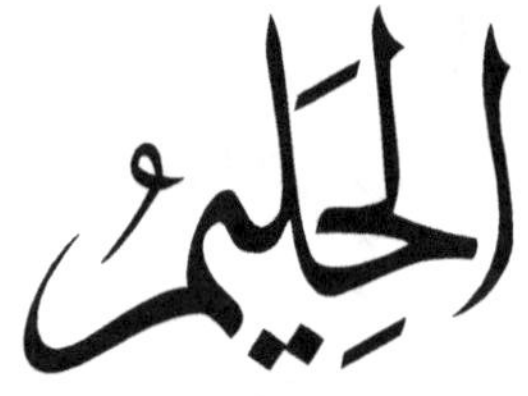

Al-Haleem

The Most Forbearing

He gives an individual respite, or time to ask Him for forgiveness. Allah is not in haste to punish an individual for his sins.

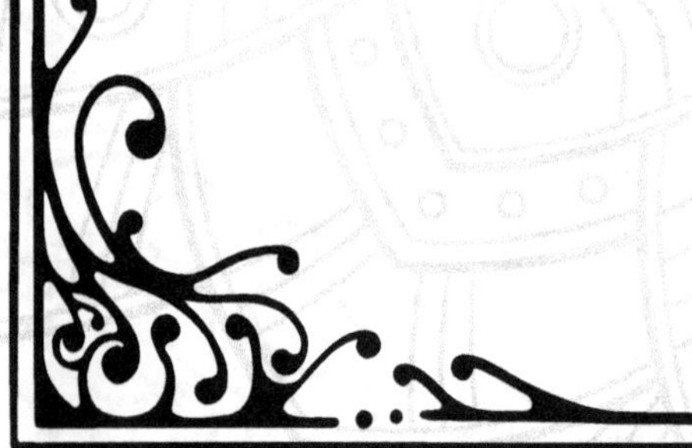

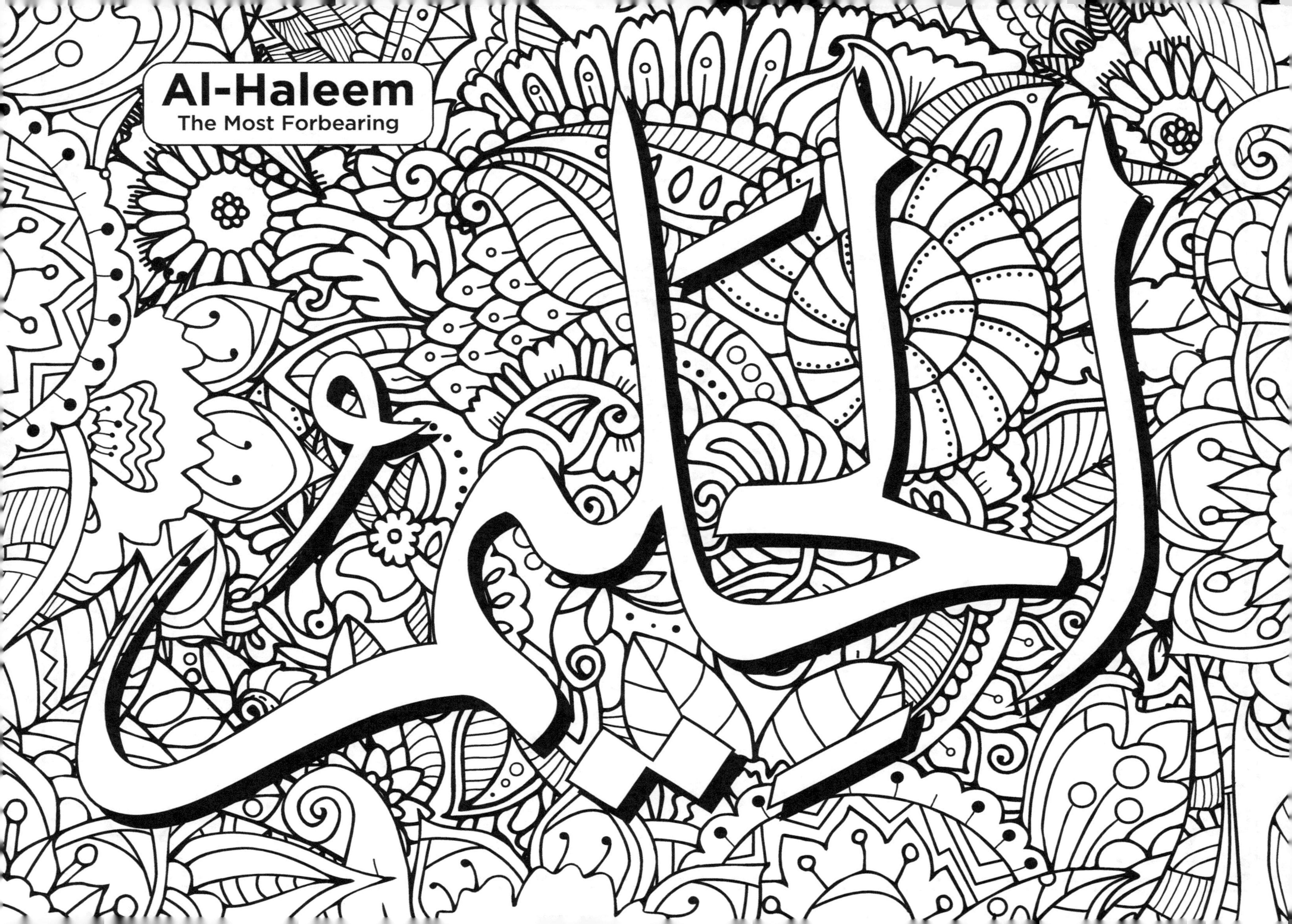
Al-Haleem
The Most Forbearing
الحليم

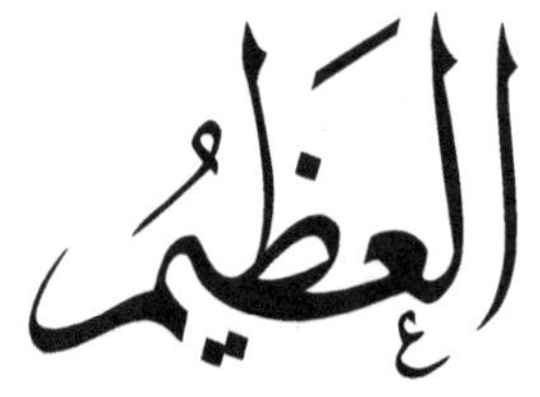

Al-Azeem

The Magnificent One

The One who is Greatest, Mightiest, Grandest and above all.

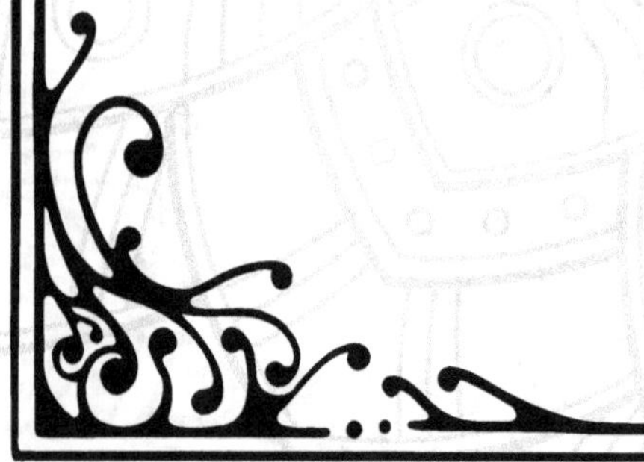

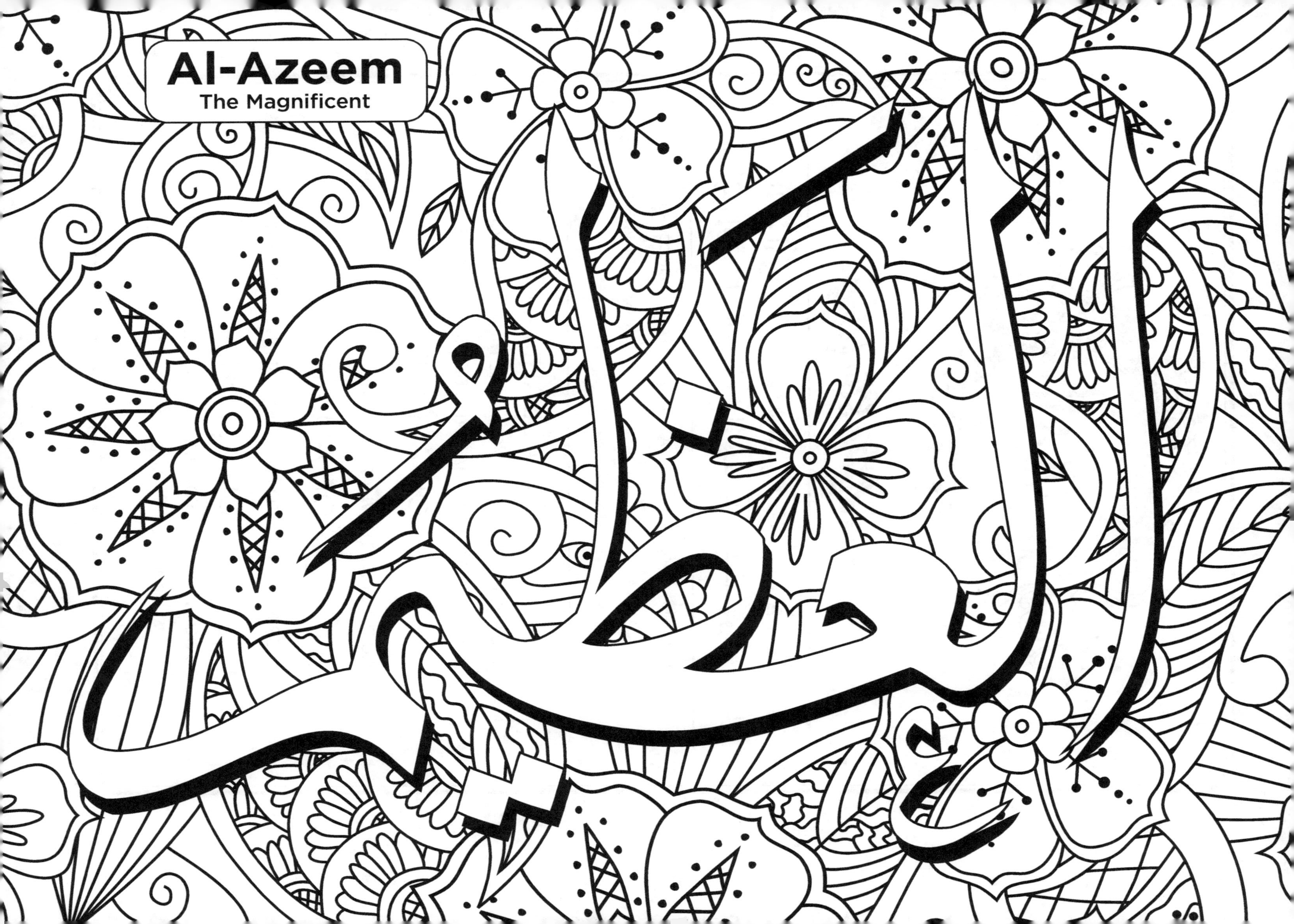
Al-Azeem
The Magnificent
العظيم

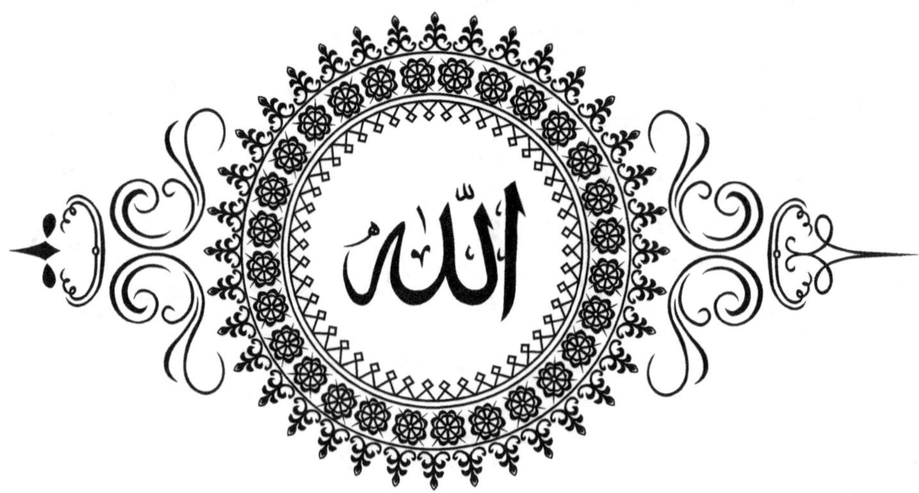

Dua After Studying

اللَّهُمَّ إِنِّي أَسْتَوْدِعُكَ مَا قَرأتُ وَمَا حَفَظْتُ، فَرُضُهُ عَليّ عِنْدَ
حَاجَتِي إِلَيهِ، إِنّكَ عَلى مَا تَشَاءُ قَدِيرُ وَأَنْتَ حَسْبِي وَنِعْمَ الوَكِيل

ALLAHUMMA INNI ASTAODEEKA MA QARA'TU WAMA HAFAZ-TU. FARUDDUHU 'ALLAYA INDA HAJATI ELAHI. INNAKA 'ALA MA-TASHA'-U QADEER WA ANTA HASBEEYA WA NA'MAL WAKEEL.

OH ALLAH!

MAKE USEFUL FOR ME WHAT YOU HAVE TAUGHT ME AND TEACH ME KNOWLEDGE THAT WILL BE USEFUL TO ME.

OH ALLAH!

I ENTRUST YOU WITH WHAT I HAVE READ AND I HAVE STUDIED.

OH ALLAH!

BRING IT BACK TO ME WHEN I AM IN NEED OF IT.

OH ALLAH!

YOU DO WHATEVER YOU WISH, YOU ARE MY AVAILER AND PROTECTOR AND THE BEST OF AID.

The 99 Attributes of Allah coloring book series will motivate you to learn, memorize and understand the meaning of Allah's attributes. The first volume contains 33 unique and beautiful names along with a variety of ornate and detailed illustrations.

There are many health benefits of adult coloring books. For example, it can reduce stress, decrease anxiety, improve motor skills, improve sleep, helps you focus and relaxes the brain.

Coloring goes beyond being a fun activity for relaxation!

We hope you find enjoyment and benefit in our coloring book series. Make sure to share them with your family and friends.

COLLECT ALL 3 VOLUMES!

Visit us at **mugirls.com** for other coloring book series.

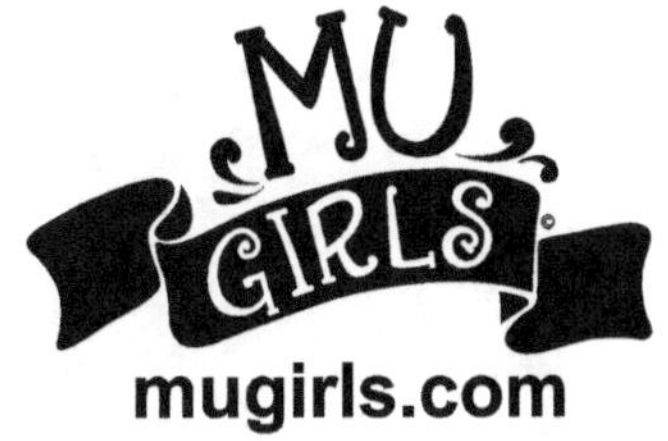

mugirls.com

www.ingramcontent.com/pod-product-compliance
Lightning Source LLC
LaVergne TN
LVHW061254100826
845148LV00008B/1120
9781736817841